ERIC VALE

SUPER MALE

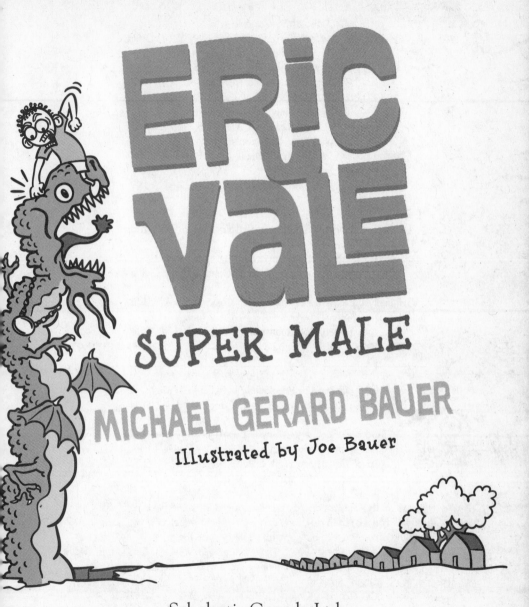

ERIC VALE

SUPER MALE

MICHAEL GERARD BAUER

Illustrated by Joe Bauer

Scholastic Canada Ltd.
Toronto New York London Auckland Sydney
Mexico City New Delhi Hong Kong Buenos Aires

Scholastic Canada Ltd.
604 King Street West, Toronto, Ontario M5V 1E1, Canada
Scholastic Inc.
557 Broadway, New York, NY 10012, USA
Scholastic Australia Pty Limited
PO Box 579, Gosford, NSW 2250, Australia
Scholastic New Zealand Limited
Private Bag 94407, Botany, Manukau 2163, New Zealand
Scholastic Children's Books
Euston House, 24 Eversholt Street, London NW1 1DB, UK

www.scholastic.ca

Library and Archives Canada Cataloguing in Publication

Bauer, Michael Gerard, 1955–, author
Eric Vale, super male / Michael Gerard Bauer ; illustrated
by Joe Bauer.
Originally published: Parkside, SA : Omnibus Books, 2013.
ISBN 978-1-4431-3935-9 (pbk.)
I. Bauer, Joe (Illustrator), illustrator II. Title.
PZ7.B322Ers 2015   j823.'92   C2014-904571-9

First published by Scholastic Australia in 2013.
This edition published by Scholastic Canada Ltd. in 2015.

6 5 4 3 2 1   Printed in Canada 139   15 16 17 18 19

For Shintaro Akikusa – my hero still – MGB
To Dad, Mum and Meg – best family ever – JB

1. He Said What?

It's Friday afternoon. I'm sitting down the back of the class minding my own business.

That's when Mr. Winter, our Year Five teacher, comes out with the **craziest thing ever.**

"On Monday, in the lead-up to our school fete and open day next weekend, we'll be starting a short study unit on ..."

Wait for it.

You **ready** for this?

Here it comes ...

"Stupid Pharaohs."

PLAGUES ARE GOOD THINGS, RIGHT?

Then, the intercom buzzes and Mr. Winter has to answer it.

Huh? What was that? Did he just say we're doing a study unit on ... **stupid** pharaohs? BUT THAT'S INSANE!

Of all the things we could study, why would Mr. Winter choose that? I mean, if we **have** to learn about people who died about a zillion years ago like the pharaohs, why couldn't he make it the smart ones or the funny ones or – and **here's** an idea – the **interesting** ones? What are we wasting our time on the **dumb** ones for?

BZZZ

SMART

FUNNY

INTERESTING

OH DEAR.

THIS SIDE UP

SAND 101

And how do you become a stupid pharaoh in the first place? Get your mummies and daddies all mixed up? Fail "Introduction to Sand" at pharaoh pre-school? Build your pyramids upside down?

No matter how you looked at it, doing a study unit on stupid pharaohs was **totally nuts!**

Of course, there was just the **teeeeeeeeeeeeeniest weeeeeeeeeeeeeniest** possibility that I might have heard that wrong. I wasn't **exactly** hanging on Mr. Winter's every word at the time. But can you **blame** me? I mean, what were the chances Mr. Winter was going to come out with something worth hearing? Anyway, back when he said ...

Well ... whatever it was that he **did** say ... I was busy doing other stuff. **Important** stuff. **Secret Agent** stuff! You see, I'd just come up with this mega-brilliant story idea for my **Totally Awesome Action Adventures of Secret Agent Derek "Danger" Dale**. Or at least I **thought** I had, until Mr. Winter blurted out that weird thing about the stupid pharaohs and then I **totally** forgot what my mega-brilliant idea was. Teachers can be so distracting! After that I couldn't get stupid pharaohs out of my head! And one thing is for sure, secret agents and stupid pharaohs just don't go together.

HELLO? I CAN'T HEAR YOU.

YES, IT'S ME.

SECRET STUPID AGENT PHARAOH

→ 4 ←

Ever!

Well ... not normally ... unless ...
I grabbed my pen and threw
open my special **Awesome Stories
and Genius Thoughts Journal.**

Secret Agent Derek
"Danger" Dale crawled down
the narrow tunnel into the
centre of the pyramid. Who
would have thought that Agent
Dale's quest to find evil Doctor
Evil MacEvilness's secret evil
headquarters would end up here
in a pharaoh's tomb?

Brilliant! I rock!

Let's seeeeeeeeeeeee now ...

The tunnel led to a large chamber. In the centre was a mummy's casket. It GLITTERED like it was TOTALLY covered in heaps and heaps of PRECIOUS JEWELS! Agent Dale shone his light on it and took a closer look. It was TOTALLY covered in heaps and heaps of WORTHLESS GLITTER!

It was also upside down. And there were smiley faces drawn on it.

Derek "Danger" Dale carefully laid the casket down and used his special edition Secret Agent Crowbar to remove the lid. A scary moan filled the room. The mummy inside sat up and started tearing bandages from its head!

"Thank goodness for *that!*" it cried out. "TALK. ABOUT. STUFFY!"

Agent Dale cleared his throat. The mummy froze then turned slowly. Two angry eyes stared at Derek.

"Who has DARED to disturb the Mightiest of the Mighties?"

"Secret Agent Derek 'Danger' Dale at your service ... but since I *am* a *secret* agent ... and it's actually supposed to be a bit of a ... *secret* ... I'd be *very* grateful if you wouldn't go blabbing it abou -"

"SILENCE! How dare you speak in my presence when you answer me!"

"But how -"

"SILENCE, I SAY! Do you not know who sits before you?"

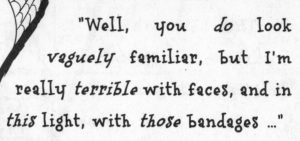

"Well, you *do* look *vaguely* familiar, but I'm really *terrible* with faces, and in *this* light, with *those* bandages ..."

The mummy glared.

"Silence?" Agent Dale asked.

The mummy glared again and rose to its full height. Which actually wasn't really very full. Or high.

"I am the MIGHTIEST of the MIGHTY pharaohs who were MIGHTILY MIGHTY. All who hear my name, tremble and shake. I am THIKASABRIKUS!"

Agent Dale began to tremble and shake. Luckily he didn't laugh out loud.

Then he frowned. "Just a second. Thikasabrikus, you say? You know, that name *does* ring a bell. I seem to recall that when I was in primary school, we did this short study unit ... something about ... the *Stupid Pharaohs?*"

I stopped writing for a moment to check on what Mr. Winter was up to. He was still talking away on the intercom. **Awesome!**

Meanwhile, back in the pharaoh's tomb ...

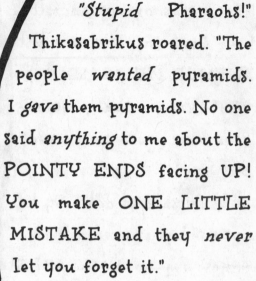

"*Stupid* Pharaohs!" Thikasabrikus roared. "The people *wanted* pyramids. I *gave* them pyramids. No one said *anything* to me about the POINTY ENDS facing UP! You make ONE LITTLE MISTAKE and they *never* let you forget it."

Secret Agent Derek "Danger" Dale stared in silence at the strange tangle of bandages before him.

"SPEAK!" the mummy demanded.

"But you just told m-"

"SILENCE! I have no time for your foolishness ...

The spirits of my ancestors have been insulted. I must AVENGE MY DEATH!"

"Avenge your death? Then you were murdered! But how?"

"Crushed to death by an upside-down pyramid. Those things are so UNSTABLE! But," Thikasabrikus said, holding up a finger, "did it just fall, or was it ... PUSHED?"

Then his eyes swept angrily around the room.

"And see how they have mocked me with worthless glitter and the shameful faces of smiliness ...

Thank goodness they didn't bury me upside down. That would have been too much!"

"Well, now that you men -"

"SILENCE, I SAY! They have dared to laugh at a pharaoh and now *all* must pay - BIG TIME!"

Thikasabrikus pulled a small leather bag from inside his bandages. It was covered in jewels and fastened with a golden clip on top.

"Do you have any idea what *this* is?"

Agent Dale cried out in horror and stepped back. "No! It can't be. Is that ..."

"Yes." Thikasabrikus grinned wickedly. "The PURSE OF THE MUMMY!"

Genius!

Better have another quick check on Mr. Winter. He was off the intercom now and back at his desk counting out a bunch of papers. Awesome! Time for just a liiiiiiiiiiiittle bit more ...

Dale's eyes narrowed. "And what are you going to do with that?"

Thikasabrikus shrugged. "DESTROY the world, what else? Inside are the two deadliest scarab beetles ever known to man."

"Or woman," Agent Dale mumbled to himself politically correctly.

"They are the dreaded SCARABS FROM HELL — a birthday present from my evil high priest Wunbaddoodis. They eat nothing but human flesh and breed like rabbits ...

In no time they will cover the entire world. Only he who sets them free is safe! Who's laughing now, eh? BWAHAHAHAHAHA! Oh, look - it's *ME!*"

Agent Derek "Danger" Dale took a pace forward.

"I'm sorry to be the one to spoil the party, O INCREDIBLY THICK ONE, but that 'destroying the world' bit you just mentioned? Well, it's NEVER GOING TO HAPPEN."

"Oh no? And who will stop me?"

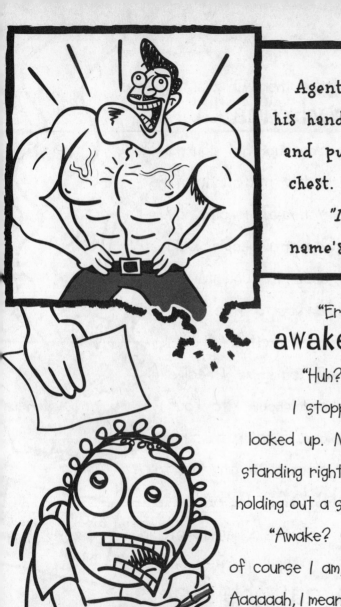

Agent Dale placed his hands on his hips and puffed out his chest.

"*I will - or my name's not -*"

"Eric Vale, are you awake?"

"Huh? What?"

I stopped writing and looked up. Mr. Winter was standing right in front of me holding out a sheet of paper!

"Awake? Oh yeah, yeah, of course I am, Mr. Mummy ... Aaaaaah, I mean Daddy ... I mean Baddie ... I mean Winter!"

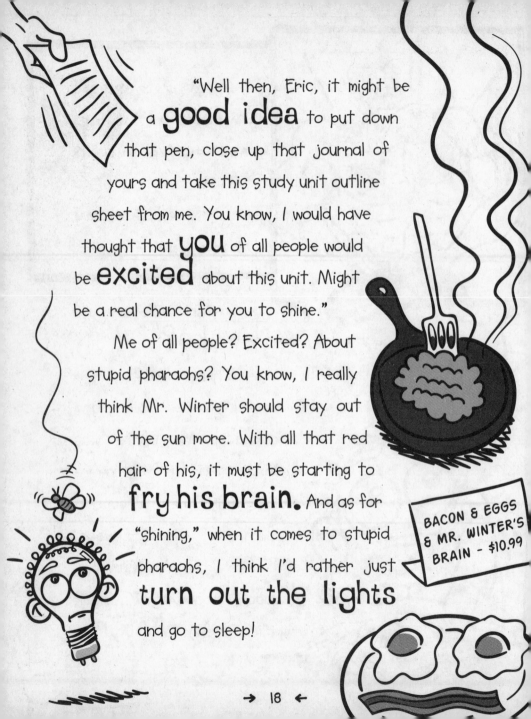

"Well then, Eric, it might be a **good idea** to put down that pen, close up that journal of yours and take this study unit outline sheet from me. You know, I would have thought that **you** of all people would be **excited** about this unit. Might be a real chance for you to shine."

Me of all people? Excited? About stupid pharaohs? You know, I really think Mr. Winter should stay out of the sun more. With all that red hair of his, it must be starting to **fry his brain.** And as for "shining," when it comes to stupid pharaohs, I think I'd rather just **turn out the lights** and go to sleep!

BACON & EGGS & MR. WINTER'S BRAIN - $10.99

I checked out Mr. Winter's face to see if maybe a **miracle** was happening and he was just **trying to be funny.** Hmmmm. That would be a DEFINITE NO. I looked instead at the unit outline sheet he'd given me. There was a big heading at the top of the page.

HUH?!? WHAT?!?

I blinked my eyes a couple of times to make sure I wasn't seeing things. But I **was** seeing things. Just not the things that I was **expecting** to see!

The heading didn't say STUPID PHARAOHS at all. What it **did** say was ...

SUPERHEROES!!!!!

I couldn't believe it. Was it possible?
Could it actually be happening? Were we about
to do a study unit on ... SOMETHING GOOD?
It just **didn't seem right.**
Last year with Mrs. McGurk in Year Four we
only ever did units on topics like "The Least
Interesting Stuff in the Known Universe."
But SUPERHEROES **rocked!**
Superheroes were one of my **most
favourite-est things** in
the whole world! I knew heaps of stuff about
superheroes! Superheroes were my special
subject! I was the **Superhero Guru!**

Mr. Winter was right. I **WAS** excited. **SUPER** excited! And when I looked around, I could tell that everyone else in the class was excited too.

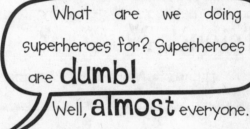

What are we doing superheroes for? Superheroes are **dumb!**

Well, **almost** everyone.

"People think super-heroes are tough and brave. But it's **easy** to act tough and brave when you've got **super powers**. I'd be brave too if I was made out of steel or I could fly or if I had **super strength** or some dumb **super shield** or **super hammer** to protect me.

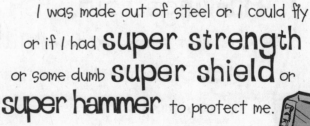

And how come superheroes just go around fighting and **smashing things up** all the time? Why don't they ever try to sit down and work things out with the bad guys so maybe they can all get along and be **friends?"**

It was Meredith Murdoch. (Who else?)

Fast-breaking News Flash!

MEREDITH MURDOCH KNOWS NOTHING ABOUT SUPERHEROES!

I'd like to see **her** sit down and have a friendly chat with a bad guy like **Humungatroid.** That dude would just smash you to a **million pieces** first and not even bother to ask any questions later!

LOOK, DISGUSTASAURUS — WHAT DO YOU SAY WE PUT ASIDE OUR DIFFERENCES AND GO FOR A NIGHT ON THE TOWN?

I was trying to explain that to Meredith, but Mr. Winter told us both to "hold those **excellent** thoughts" till next week when "everyone would get a chance to express their opinion" on the topic. And then he said this: "Even though next week will be **Superhero Week,** we'll be looking at 'real-life' heroes as well. But first, we'll start off by discussing what we **mean** by superheroes and what things they have in common. So what I'd like you all to do over the weekend is to start thinking of any superheroes

AWWWWWW...

you know, and on Monday, if you want to, you can get up and tell us all about your **favourite superhero** and why you think they're **the best.** Oh, and bring along photographs or drawings or superhero figurines if you like."

How **awesome** was that! I knew straightaway who I was going to bring to class on Monday to talk about.

Only the **coolest** superhero **ever!**

2. The Nuclear Ninjarator

I used to think **Batman** was the coolest superhero ever. But the **Nuclear Ninjarator** is even cooler! I mean, come on – a half **ninja**, half **robot** with tons of **magic** spells and **tricks**, and heaps of nuclear-powered swords and star knives? What's not to like!

For my last birthday Mum and Dad got me this **awesome** Nuclear Ninjarator action figure with all the accessories and attachments.

HEIGHT COMPARISON

- Hobbit
- Leprechaun
- Gremlin
  CHEWY
- Thumbelina

That's what I was putting together on Saturday afternoon when my **best friend** William "Choo-Choo" Rodriguez called around. "Chewy" for short. (Which he is.)

"Wow, the Ninj is looking **great**, Eric!"

"Yeah, I can't wait to give my talk on Monday."

"Me either."

"Really? You're doing a talk? Who on?"

Chewy took a big piece of paper from his pocket, unfolded it and held it up in front of me.

There was a picture on it that I'm fairly sure was drawn by Chewy himself.

→ 26 ←

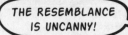

THE RESEMBLANCE
IS UNCANNY!

It looked a lot like him in **tights**
and **a cape** and wearing a
swimming cap on his head that had
the letters MSB on it. Either that
or it was a **bald monkey**
with a tattooed forehead playing
dressing up. Below the picture was a
name printed in big letters.

"Mr. Self-Belief?"

Chewy grinned and bobbed
his head up and down **like a
jackhammer.**

"He's a superhero?"

More grinning and bobbing from Chewy.

"But I've never heard of him."

"He's the **best,** Eric! My dad's
told me lots of stories about him."

"Riiiiiiiiiiiiiiiiight."

It was all beginning to make sense now. You see, Chewy's mum and dad are motivational speakers and life coaches. They're right into POSITIVE thinking and BELIEVING in yourself and stuff like that. Their latest book is called **YOU Can Be POSITIVELY Great!** Chewy's parents are really nice people. They're always happy and smiling. Always. It's a **bit scary.**

"Mr. Self-Belief is so cool, Eric. See, **normally,** he's just this ordinary kid called Wally Ramirez."

"Hey, what do you know? Same initials as you! Even sounds a bit the same. William Rodriguez — Wally Ramirez."

"Heeeeeeeeey, yeeeeeeeeeeaaaah. Never noticed that before. Well, anyway, the thing is, Wally doesn't always stay Wally. He changes! Like there was this **one** story my dad told me where Wally was **trapped** on the top of a **burning skyscraper** and the only way he could save himself was by jumping across to the roof of the next building. But guess what, Eric? It was waaaaaaaay too far and Wally didn't think he could do it!"

"Uh-huh. So what happened?"

"Well, it was looking really bad for Wally. But then, all of a sudden, he like, stopped doubting himself and started **believing** that he could do it and then, just like magic, he turns into Mr. Self-Belief and he just jumps right across, no problems at all!"

I BELIEVE!

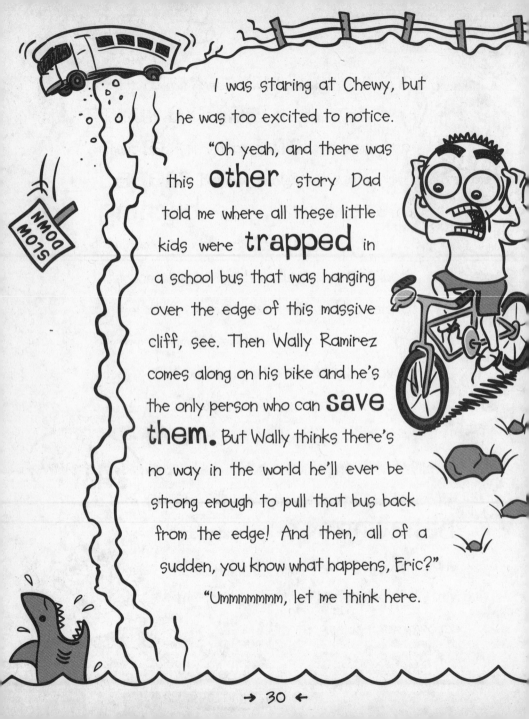

I was staring at Chewy, but he was too excited to notice.

"Oh yeah, and there was this **other** story Dad told me where all these little kids were **trapped** in a school bus that was hanging over the edge of this massive cliff, see. Then Wally Ramirez comes along on his bike and he's the only person who can **save them.** But Wally thinks there's no way in the world he'll ever be strong enough to pull that bus back from the edge! And then, all of a sudden, you know what happens, Eric?"

"Ummmmmmm, let me think here.

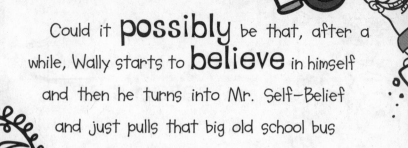

Could it **possibly** be that, after a while, Wally starts to **believe** in himself and then he turns into Mr. Self-Belief and just pulls that big old school bus filled with little kids to safety?"

"Wow! That's amazing! How did you **know** that? Has my dad told you that story too?"

"No. Just a lucky guess."

"That's incredible! I can't believe you just guessed that. But it shows how you **never** know what can happen. Just like the time Wally Ramirez didn't believe he had a **chance** of winning the World Heavyweight Boxing title because, you know, he's just a kid and everything, but then ..."

I AIM TO PLEASE.

The door of my room swung open and **saved me.**

"What are you and Chewy pwaying, Wicky? Can I pway too? Can I, Wicky? Can I pway what you and Chewy are pwaying? Can I pwease? Can I pway too?"

Almost saved me. It was my little sister Katie.

"We're not **playing** anything, Katie. We're doing **important big-school** stuff. Stuff you wouldn't understand because you're too little. So why don't you go back to your own room now and just leave us alone, okay?"

Katie **stared** at me with big eyes.

They started to blink.

Oh-no.

Then her mouth turned into an upside-down horseshoe and her bottom lip pushed out like **a helicopter landing pad.**

OH-NO!

And her chin began to **wobble!**

OH-NOOOOOOOOOOOOOOOO!

She was changing, just like Wally Ramirez! Only she wasn't changing into a superhero. She was changing into KATIE the KRAZY KRYING KID!

I had to stop her or I'd get into **big trouble** from Mum and Dad.

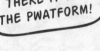

THERE IT IS! THE PWATFORM!

"No, Katie. Wait. Don't cry. I was just kiddin." Really. Of **course** you can stay if you want to ...

→ 33 ←

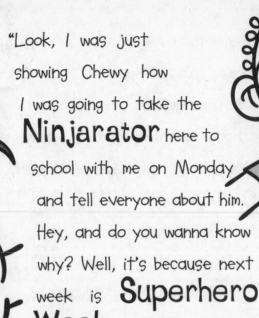

"Look, I was just showing Chewy how I was going to take the **Ninjarator** here to school with me on Monday and tell everyone about him. Hey, and do you wanna know why? Well, it's because next week is **Superhero Week.** That's right! It's going to be all about superheroes, and we're allowed to bring our favourite superheroes to school. Isn't that **great?**"

Katie sniffed a couple of times. Her mouth and lip went back to normal. She wiped her nose on the back of her hand. She smiled. PHEW!

Then she ran out of the room. Chewy and I looked at each other and shrugged. A few seconds later Katie was back. And she was dragging something behind her. She held it up with a big grin.

"Woopsie Bear's the **bestest** Snooperherwo ever!"

Correction: Woopsie Bear is **nothing** like a superhero at all.

What Woopsie Bear happens to be, is Katie's **favourite** toy in the entire world, and she's had him ever since she was born.

Except he looked a lot different then. You see, what Katie **doesn't** know is that one day our dog Barkley went **nutso** and tore Woopsie Bear

and another one of Katie's stuffed toys **totally to pieces.** The problem was, there weren't enough good bits to fix them both. We think Barkley must have **swallowed** a fair bit. So, because Woopsie Bear was Katie's favourite, Mum decided to try to put him back together using some of the stuffing and **leftover bits** from the other toy. Which would have been a **good idea** if the other toy hadn't been Orville the Orange Orangutan.

So that's how come Woopsie Bear has one small eye and one big eye, these **really** long arms, and looks more like **roadkill** than a cuddly toy. Mum told Katie that Woopsie had been given **"a bit of a makeover"** and that he grew his arms long so that he could give her "bigger hugs." Guess what? Katie **totally bought it!** Plus, she loved Woopsie even more now because he had these Velcro paws, which meant she could hang him around her neck.

"Aaaah, Katie ... Look ... ummm ... Woopsie's **great** and all ... but I don't think he's **actually** a superhero, do you? Like he doesn't really have any special powers, does he? And he doesn't go around saving people either."

"HE DOES SO TOO! HE DOES
SO TOO! Woopsie gives special
snooper-duper
hugs that make you happy when
you're all sad ... and, and, and ...
when it's weeeeeally **dark
and spooky,** Woopsie
Bear chases all the naughty bad
spooky-spooks away!"

"**Really?**" Chewy said.
"That is **SO** cool!"

I stared at him again. I did that
a lot. Katie went over and bounced
Woopsie up and down on Chewy's lap.
They were both **laughing.**

"See, Wicky. Chewy wikes Woopsie.
You should take Woopsie Bear to school
wiff you and tell all about **him.**"

PRESENT!

"WHAT! Get serious. No **way** am I taking a stupid stuffed bear to school! That's just ..."

Katie was looking at me again.

Uh-oh.

"W-W-What did you call Woopsie Bear **stoopid** for, Wicky? **Don't you wike** Woopsie Bear? (Blinking eyes!) Why don't you **wike** Woopsie Bear, Wicky? (Horseshoe mouth and landing-pad lip!) Woopsie Bear **wikes you,** Wicky. Why are you being so **m-m-mean** to him?" (Wobbly chin!)

→ 39 ←

"No, no, no, no, Katie! Wait, wait, wait! Don't cry, don't cry! I didn't mean it. I was **just joking!** I **do** like Woopsie. Of course I do. I LOVE him! Who wouldn't? And he's such a great superhero. The **best** ever! Much better than the wimpy Ninjarator. Everybody knows that! I was just telling Chewy the same thing before you came in. And I was even saying how **awesome** it would be if I could take Woopsie to school with me next week."

Chewy's face twisted up in a frown.

"I don't remem –"

"Yes, that's **right,** Chewy! And remember how I also told you that the reason

I **couldn't** take Woopsie to school with me was because Katie needed him at home to give her all those special super-duper hugs and to keep away all the spooky-spook guys? See, Katie? So **that's** why I'm taking my **second**-favourite superhero to school, even though Woopsie would obviously be **SOOOOOOO** much better. Oh, well. Not to worry. I'll survive ... somehow."

Oh, brother! The things you have to do when you have a little sister.

SPOOKY-SPOOK
spookus spookaenius

Katie sucked her bottom lip back in. "Is that **twue**, Wicky?"

"True? Sure! Absolutely! Definitely! Of course!"

SPOOKY
SPOOK

(It's not really a lie if it's to stop your little sister crying, is it?)

"Well, if you really ..."

But now someone was calling from outside. It was Mum.

"Katie! Katie, sweetheart, where are you? Come on, I want you to try on these new clothes I bought you."

Katie's mouth dropped open. "Bye!" she said, and ran off.

I went over to shut the door. "Phew, **that was close.**

Almost had the major waterworks – twice! Can you believe Katie actually thought I'd want to take some dumb bear to school? I don't know how she can even **touch** that **freaky thing,** do you, Chewy?" There was no answer.

I turned round. Chewy looked up at me.

"Sorry? What was that, Eric?"

"Aaaaaaah ... nothing. Nothing at all."

Woopsie Bear was hanging off the side of his face. Its arms were wrapped around his forehead like a headband. Chewy was grinning insanely. He gave me the thumbs up.

"Velcro paws. Wick-**ed!**"

3. A Super Surprise!

By Sunday night the **Nuclear Ninjarator** was all ready to go, so I put him in a shoebox with a bit of bubble wrap and left it out on the kitchen table where I ate breakfast. That way I knew I wouldn't forget to take it the next day.

Of course in class on Monday morning **everyone** wanted to know what I had in the shoebox. But **no way** would I tell them. It was going to be a big surprise!

I AM SO BRAVE.

SNAKE EYES AGAIN?

And they'd have to wait too because I wasn't the only one doing a talk. Heaps of kids had brought along action figures and posters and lots of other **superhero stuff** as well. So Mr. Winter put all our names in a hat to work out the order of the talks.

The presentations were a lot of fun. Everyone was enjoying them. Except maybe for Meredith Murdoch. (Who else?) She just kept **rolling her eyes** all the time and saying stuff like, "He gets to hide inside a **humungous** iron robot suit! What's brave about that?"

Anyway, it was almost morning tea when Mr. Winter said, "Time for just one more before the break. And that **lucky** person is ... Eric Vale."

I **jumped** out of my seat and headed out to the front of the class. Chewy came along with me. He'd volunteered to be my assistant. Just like he'd volunteered to **guard** the Nuclear Ninjarator for me all morning until it was time for my talk. Chewy loves volunteering for stuff.

When we got out the front, Chewy put the shoebox on the teacher's desk. Then he tilted up the lid on one side so no one else could see, and took **a quick peek** inside to check that everything was all right. He launched one of his biggest smiles and gave me a **thumbs up.**

Time for my presentation to begin!

"Mr. Winter and 5W, we heard about some pretty good superheroes already, but now I'm going to tell you all about the NEWEST

and COOLEST SUPERHERO EVER! If some bad guy like Humungatroid or even The Megamaniac was trying to **destroy the world** or if you were being attacked by something like a killer, mutant, **alien monster,** this is **definitely** the guy you should call for help. He's smart, he's tricky, he's brave (insert Meredith Murdoch eye roll here), and he always beats the baddies."

'MUTANT'? HARSH.

I nod at Chewy, who shoves his hand inside the shoebox and then nods back at me.

"Here he is. He's my new, very favourite superhero, and I'm sure he'll soon be yours as well. His name is ..."

This is where Chewy whips out the Nuclear Ninjarator and holds him with both hands high above his head so **everyone** can see him while I call out his name. But the only problem is, when I look up, it's not the Nuclear Ninjarator that Chewy's holding up above his head!

My brain **freezes.**

"... aaaaaaaaaa ..."

I can't think.

"... aaaaaaaaaa ..."

I can't speak.

"... aaaaaaaaaa ..."

But Chewy can.

"It's SUPER WOOPSIE BEAR!" he shouts.

And before I know it there's all this laughing and pointing, and some

BRAIN NEW FLAVOUR!

of the girls are smiling and giggling and saying stuff like, "He's so sweeeeeeeeeeeeet!" and "Awwwwww, how cuuuuuuute!" Then I see Martin Fassbender and Tyrone Knowles. They're laughing so hard I think their faces might **split in half.** (No such luck.) Sophie Peters is blushing. Meredith Murdoch is just **staring** at me from behind her glasses and **frowning.**

It takes **ages** for Mr. Winter to quieten everyone down. Then I try to explain what must have happened. How my little sister must have swapped her stupid bear for the Nuclear Ninjarator when I wasn't looking because she thought she was helping me out.

I tell them that "no way is Woopsie Bear my favourite superhero!" but Martin just cracks everyone up by asking me, "Who is it, then? **Super Dolly-Wolly?"**

Luckily the bell rings then for morning tea. Mr. Winter says I can have another go tomorrow if I want to. He tells me not to worry about it and that it just shows how superheroes can come in "many shapes and sizes."

Yes, sure, just like **total losers** can.

When everyone else piles outside, I stay in the classroom. So does Chewy. I thump my head on the desk and groan. The first day of **SUPERHERO WEEK** is a **SUPER DISASTER!**

Then I suddenly remember something and sit up.

"Hey, wait a minute. You looked in the shoebox."

Chewy nodded.

"Before I even started my talk, you looked in the shoebox."

Chewy nodded again.

"You gave me the **thumbs up.**"

Chewy nodded some more.

"Well ... why didn't you **say** something? Why didn't you **warn** me?"

Chewy wrinkled up his nose and thought about my questions carefully before he answered.

"Warn you about **what?**"

"About what? About what do you **think?** About Woopsie Bear being in there instead of the Ninjarator!"

"I thought you put him in there."

"What? Me? ME! Why would I put him there? Why would you think that?"

"Because on Saturday you said that Woopsie was your **favourite** superhero and the Nuclear Ninjarator was your **second**-favourite. Isn't that what you said?"

"Yes, I **said** it, but I didn't **mean** it! I was just saying that so Katie wouldn't get all upset and cry. How could you think that was true? How could you **possibly** think that my favourite superhero would be a MANGY, BUG-EYED, DOPEY, MUTANT, FREAKY-LOOKING ORANGUTAN BEAR?"

Chewy's eyes widened. He **stared** at me.

Something about that look was familiar.

"Why are you being so mean?" Chewy said. "Don't you **like** Woopsie Bear, Eric?"

I waited.

If he blinked just once, I was going to **strangle him** with Woopsie's orangutan arms!

o•o•o•o•o•o•o•o•o•o•

That afternoon when I got home, Katie was **bouncing around** everywhere. She wanted to hear all about Woopsie Bear's "big school-day adventure."

"Did you wike my surpwise, Wicky? Did you? Huh? Did you, Wicky?"

"Oh ... um yeah ...Yeah, Katie ... it was just ... so **great.** Never been more surprised in all my life. But look, if you're ever thinking of doing something like that again, why don't you tell me about it first, okay?"

"Ha, that's **silly!** Then it wouldn't be a surpwise."

"Hmmmmm. Yes. **What a shame** that would be."

I went to my room. I decided to write some more of my Derek "Danger" Dale story to take my mind off the Woopsie **disaster.** But Katie followed me in.

"Hey, Wicky, you wanna pway a game with me and Woopsie? 'Cause Woopsie's your fav-vite, isn't he? Do you, huh? You wanna pway a game wiff us?"

I'M ALL IN.

T.A.A.A.
S.A.D.D.D.

YEEHAW!

"Aaaah ... Not reeeeeeeeeeeally."

I sat down at my desk and pulled my journal from my bag. I opened it up and found the last bit I'd written in the **Totally Awesome Action Adventures of Secret Agent Derek "Danger" Dale.**

"You wanna pway sompink else, then? You wanna pway with me and my Pwecious Pwincess Pony-Wony ponies? I got six now! If I get **one** more I'll have ten!"

6 + 1
= 10

"Right. Well, that sounds like awesome fun, Katie, but you see I'm preeeeeetty busy right at the moment, so maybe some other time."

"You want a Pwecious Pwincess Pony-Wony Good Luck tattoo then?

ANY QUESTIONS?

→ 55 ←

Do you, Wicky? I got pwenty. You want one, Wicky? You want a Pwecious Pwincess Pony-Wony Good Luck tattoo? You can have one, if you want one. You weally can. If you want."

PONY, HUH? 'GOOD LUCK' STAYING ALIVE.

"Okay, okay. Look. If I take a tattoo, will you **promise** to go and play by yourself – in **your** room – and let me write my story?"

"Uh-huh. Sure!"

"Okay, it's a deal."

Katie ran off. I started to read over my last Secret Agent Derek "Danger" Dale entry. I didn't get too far before a hand was shoved under my face.

"Here!"

GOOD LUCK!

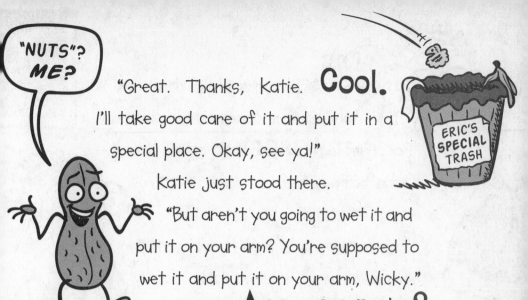

"NUTS"? **ME?**

"Great. Thanks, Katie. **Cool.** I'll take good care of it and put it in a special place. Okay, see ya!"

ERIC'S SPECIAL TRASH

Katie just stood there.

"But aren't you going to wet it and put it on your arm? You're supposed to wet it and put it on your arm, Wicky."

"What? **Are you nuts?** No way am I having a Pony-Wony tattoo **anywhere** on my body!"

Everything went quiet. I looked at Katie.

O-oh.

Big eyes ... Check! ✓

Blinking ... Check! ✓

Upside-down horseshoe mouth ... Check! ✓

Landing-pad lip ... Check! ✓

Wobbly chin ... Check! ✓

Prague ... Czech! ✓

"Quick, Katie! What are you waiting for? Get me some water! I wanna stick this **awesome** tattoo somewhere on my body!"

And I did.

But way up high on my left shoulder where my shirt sleeve would totally cover it up until I could have my shower and scrub it off. (Don't worry, I checked the packet – **Washes off in water. Sweet!**)

Katie left and **finally** I was alone with my journal.

But it didn't help much. I tried to write something, but I couldn't stop thinking about what had happened at school that day.

GOOD LUCK!

~ Washes off in water ... Check!

ERIC'S MIND

Once upon a Woopsie

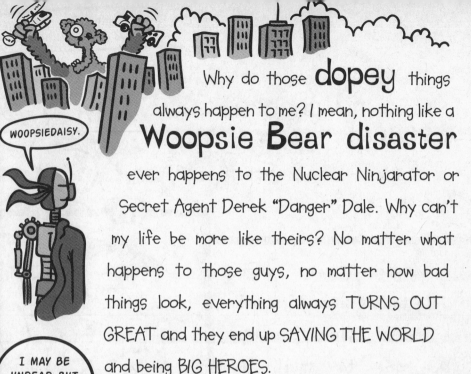

WOOPSIEDAISY.

I MAY BE UNDEAD, BUT THE "PSYCHO" IS UNCALLED FOR.

WELL, IT SURE BEATS HELL.

Why do those **dopey** things always happen to me? I mean, nothing like a **Woopsie Bear disaster** ever happens to the Nuclear Ninjarator or Secret Agent Derek "Danger" Dale. Why can't my life be more like theirs? No matter what happens to those guys, no matter how bad things look, everything always TURNS OUT GREAT and they end up SAVING THE WORLD and being BIG HEROES.

Like, right now in my story, Secret Agent Derek "Danger" Dale is stuck inside this pyramid in Egypt with a psycho, **undead mummy** who's about to release two **deadly scarabs** from hell to go on a human **flesh-eating** pig-out and **destroy the entire world.**

So you'd probably think that Agent Dale's got **no chance,** right? Well, think again.

Let's just recap a little first before going on ...

HEY! THESE ARE THE SAME CARTOONS FROM BEFORE!

Agent Derek "Danger" Dale took a pace forward.

"I'm sorry to be the one to spoil the party, O INCREDIBLY THICK ONE, but that 'destroying the world' bit you just mentioned? Well, it's NEVER GOING TO HAPPEN."

"Oh no? And who will stop me?"

Agent Dale placed his hands on his hips and puffed out his chest.

"*I* will, or my name's not Secret Agent Der - No, wait! Thought you could fool me a second time, eh? Well, I'm not telling you my name again, because it's a secret!"

Thikasabrikus laughed and held out the jewel-covered purse. He clicked it open.

"You have uttered your last foolish words, Secret Agent Cedric 'Stranger' Stale!"

"Ha! Not even close, THICK BRICK! It's Secret Agent DEREK 'DANGER' DALE, if you must know ... Uh-oh ... Wait a minute ... CURSES!"

"Well, *now* you've uttered your last foolish words. Prepare to be first course for the hellish scarabs FROM HELL!"

Thikasabrikus laughed. "BWHAHAHAHAHAHA!"

Then he upended the deadly purse over Agent Dale's head.

A trickle of dust poured out.

Thikasabrikus's jaw fell open. "But where are my hellish scarabs from hell? Snoogie! Sabu! My babies! What has happened to you?"

Derek coughed and shook a cloud of dust from his hair.

"Well, Your Thickness, it *has* been a few thousand years since they've had a meal of human flesh. Perhaps you should have left some *finger* food for them?"

Thikasabrikus turned pale. "A few thousand years? I thought I'd just dropped off for a couple of hours. No wonder my throat feels so ... *dry.*"

And with that, the mighty Pharaoh Thikasabrikus, who claimed to be the mightiest of all the mighty pharaohs who were mightily mighty, but who in fact was mightily mistaken, cracked down the middle, shattered into a thousand pieces and crumbled into a pile of dusty dust.

Secret Agent Derek "Danger" Dale brushed a speck of dirt from his shoulder, wiped his sweaty brow, smoothed his pointy moustache and flashed his winning smile.

"Well, that was a close one. For a moment there I really thought I was a goner. But what do you know? It looks like everything's TURNED OUT GREAT and I've ended up SAVING THE WORLD and being a BIG HERO - YET AGAIN!"

WHAT ABOUT ME!

See what I mean?

It just wasn't fair! And it's not that I don't want Agent Dale to win and beat the bad guys and everything, but why can't I ever get the chance to do something like that too? Why can't I be a hero for once and save the world or maybe even rescue someone from some kind of a giant beast thing? Someone who really needed my help. Someone like ...

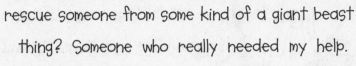

SOPHIE PETERS!

Ummmm ... Well ... not that I'm saying there's anything **special** about Sophie Peters. No way! I was just sort of picking a name and Sophie Peters just **happened** to be the first one I picked. I just meant that it would be good to rescue someone **like** Sophie Peters. Not **necessarily** Sophie Peters herself. Although of course, **if** Sophie Peters was in some kind of trouble

LOVE HEART
CONTACT LENSES

TAKE *THAT*,
GIANT BEAST
THING!

and **had** to be rescued and I was just standing around somewhere nearby **anyway,** then it would certainly be **good** to rescue her. And not just because I was rescuing Sophie Peters either. I mean, it would be good to rescue **anyone.** And that anyone of course **could** be Sophie Peters. Not that there's anything **especially** special about her!

There. I hope I've cleared that up for you.

I slammed my journal shut and started to get ready for bed. Who was I kidding? I'm PLAIN OLD Eric Vale and I'm in PLAIN OLD Year Five at PLAIN OLD Moreton Hill Primary School. I wasn't a superhero and my life wasn't an action adventure story.

No way would I ever get the chance to be like the Nuclear Ninjarator and rescue someone like (but not necessarily **actually**) Sophie Peters from some kind of a giant beast thing. In the words of Secret Agent Derek "Danger" Dale, "it's NEVER GOING TO HAPPEN!"

Except this time he was wrong.

Because the very next day at school, I got the chance to rescue Sophie Peters from some kind of a giant beast thing.

I WISH *I* WAS NUCLEAR AND TRAINED IN THE MARTIAL ARTS.

YOU. ARE. WEL. COM. **EXTERMINATE!!** >COUGH< PARDON ME.

4. Eric Vale - Super Male to the Rescue!

It started out like a pretty normal day.

First up I got to do my proper talk on the Nuclear Ninjarator. That went okay, I guess, **except** Martin Fassbender and Tyrone Knowles kept putting me off by holding up these bits of paper when Mr. Winter couldn't see them with stuff like,

"WHERE'S WOOPSIE?," "WOOPSIE BEAR FOR PRESIDENT!" and "WE LOVE WOOPSIE!" written on them.

How **hilarious** is that?

Then after morning tea we started working in groups making a list of all the things superheroes have in common. Our group was me (Woopsie Bear **loser**), Chewy **(crazy** best friend), Big Bob (class captain), Li Wan (class **brain** and really nice person) and Meredith Murdoch (no comment).

This is what we came up with for our list.

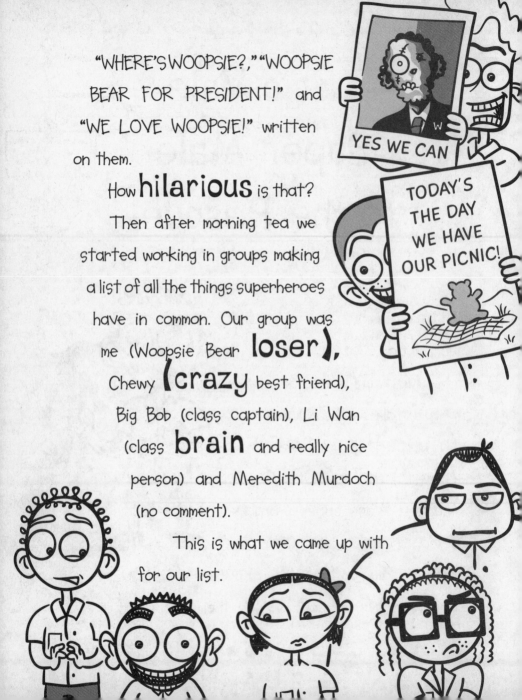

YES WE CAN

TODAY'S THE DAY WE HAVE OUR PICNIC!

Superheroes:

- Have super powers
- Wear cool costumes
- Are brave and strong (Meredith Murdoch disagrees). (Who else!)  
- Use special weapons and **gadgets** to help them fight the bad guys
- Are normal people most of the time with a **secret identity**  
- Get their super powers after **something weird happens** to them 
- Fight super bad guy enemies
- Rescue people and save the world.

IT'S **SNOW**TIME!

SUPERHERO

SECRET IDENTITY

OW!

"BAD" IS A RELATIVE TERM.

→ 71 ←

Meredith wanted to add, "Are DUMB!" but she was **outvoted.**

It was at lunchtime when I was heading back to the classroom to get a tennis ball from my bag so Chewy and I could play handball that this happened.

"Eric, can you help us – please!"

It was ...

SOPHIE PETERS!

She was just inside our classroom. Li Wan and Aasha Alsufi were behind her. They were all squeezed together in a little group. They **looked scared.**

"Who? What? **Me?**

Save? You? Now? Sure!"

For some reason I could only speak in single-word sentences.

Sophie Peters pointed to the back of the room.

"There's a **creepy-crawly** thing on the side of the lockers!" All the girls **shivered** and squashed even closer together. "We can't get our stuff."

All right! Stand back! You came to the right guy! I collect CREEPY-CRAWLY things! I'm **totally cool** with CREEPY-CRAWLY things! I **love** CREEPY-CRAWLY things!

Lizards, frogs, toads – NO PROBLEMO!

Beetles, bugs, moths, caterpillars, butterflies, crickets, **centipedes, cockroaches,** you name it – EASY PEASY! This looks like a job for **ERIC VALE - SUPER MALE!**

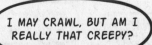

I MAY CRAWL, BUT AM I REALLY THAT CREEPY?

THERE HE IS!
GRASSZILLA!

Just as long as the creepy-crawly thing isn't a gras –

"I think it's a GRASSHOPPER! A **GIANT** ONE!"

Uh-oh. Hold the phone. Might be a **slight** PROBLEMO here. You see, I have this **thing** about grasshoppers. Yes, I know it sounds a little bit weird, but grasshoppers aren't like other creepy-crawlies. For a start, they don't really creepy-crawl, do they? They JUMP RIGHT AT YOU AND TRY TO **SCRATCH YOUR FACE OFF!**

And have you actually ever seen a picture of a grasshopper up close? Well, they've got these crazy, giant, GOGGLE EYES that stare at you like a **psycho robot**

"GOGGLE EYES"?
WELL I NEVER.

→ 74 ←

and they've got these big, **sharp,** SPIKY LEGS and CRUNCHING **alien-type jaws** and their bodies are all HARD LIKE ARMOUR and ... EEEEEEEEWWWWWWW!

I blame my mum for my thing about grasshoppers. Way back when I was just a little kid I was playing outside and I didn't want to wear my cap but Mum made me. Anyway, my cap was lying on the grass under a bush, so I just picked it up and put it on. **Something spiky** started bouncing around and **digging into my head!** I whipped off my cap and looked inside. I saw a BIG, UGLY, BROWN GRASSHOPPER! I SCREAMED.

YEAH, YOU'RE RIGHT. IT DOESN'T FIT ME.

YIPPY-KI-YAAAAAY!

The grasshopper JUMPED. My mouth was WIDE OPEN and ...

Well, let's just say it wasn't a good day for me or the grasshopper.

"Are you okay, Eric? You look a bit **sick.** We can get Mr. Winter to help if you want."

"What? No. No, I'm fine. Great. Couldn't be better!"

The girls moved away from the door and I stepped inside the classroom. The lockers were down the back. I led the way as all four of us crept a bit closer.

"THERE!" Aasha Alsufi shouted, almost **scaring me half to death.** She was pointing at some spiky legs poking around the side of the last locker.

Then they crawled around to the front. They brought **a giant spiky body** with them.

It was a grasshopper, all right. Big and green. The BIGGEST and GREENEST one ever. It was THE **INCREDIBLE HULK** OF GRASSHOPPERS!

HULK REALLY BUGGED!

"Do you think you can get it, Eric?" It was Sophie. She was looking at me with these cute ... errr, I mean ... **big, frightened** eyes.

"What? **That** little guy. Sure thing. Piece of cake. Absolutely. Not a problem. Everything's under control. I'm good to go. No worries. Easy pea – "

"But what are you going to **do?**"

PIECE OF CAKE, HUH?

"Me? Do? Ummmmmmm. Well, I could just **grab him,** of course ...

→ 77 ←

"You know, pick him up with my fingers ...
(SHUDDDDDDDDDDDDDER!) ... but I don't
want to hurt him."

Li Wan put her hands over her
mouth. "Oh, Eric, no, please don't hurt
him! It's **not his fault** he's
in the wrong place. He's probably
more frightened of us than we are
of him. And he's so beautiful!"

THE LITTLE
LADY IS RIGHT.
ALAS, BEAUTY
IS ONLY
EXOSKELETON-
DEEP.

Him? Frightened? Beautiful?
He's a SPIKY, PSYCHO, **MOUTH
INVADER!**

All right. Okay. I probably needed to
calm down a bit. Time to switch to
superhero mode. Right, here goes. Like I said,
it's ERIC VALE – SUPER MALE to the rescue!

"Okay, why don't you guys wait behind those
desks where you'll be safe and out of the way ...

and what I'll do is ... I'll take this ... aaaah ... ruler ... and I'll just go up to the locker ... and get him to **jump out** that open window that's right beside him there. That way I ... um ... he won't get hurt. How's that sound?"

"Like a plan," Sophie Peters said.

And it did. A SUPERHERO–type plan!

So Sophie, Aasha and Li crouched down behind a couple of desks with just their heads and hands poking up.

"Good luck," Li said.

"Be careful," Sophie said.

"I'm scaaaaaaared," Aasha said.

You're scared! I'm taking on a killer beast with just a **plastic ruler!**

I began edging my way closer to the lockers. I kept telling myself I could do this.

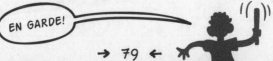
EN GARDE!

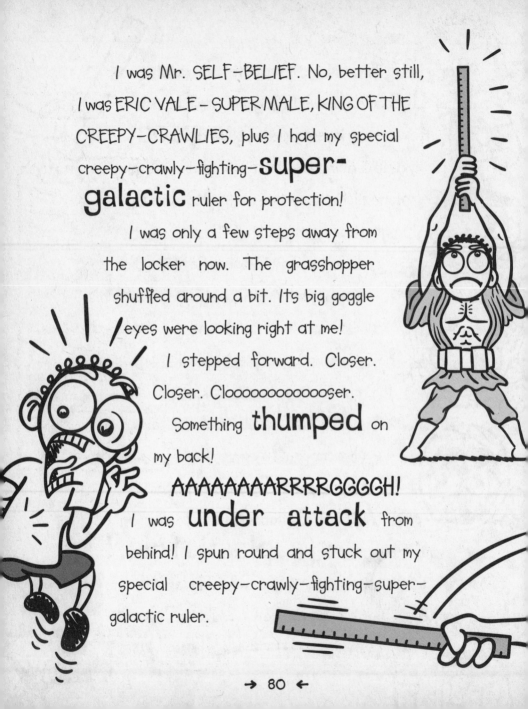

I was Mr. SELF-BELIEF. No, better still, I was ERIC VALE - SUPER MALE, KING OF THE CREEPY-CRAWLIES, plus I had my special creepy-crawly-fighting-**super-galactic** ruler for protection!

I was only a few steps away from the locker now. The grasshopper shuffled around a bit. Its big goggle eyes were looking right at me!

I stepped forward. Closer. Closer. Cloooooooooooooser.

Something **thumped** on my back!

AAAAAAAARRRRGGGGH!

I was **under attack** from behind! I spun round and stuck out my special creepy-crawly-fighting-super-galactic ruler.

"Hey, Eric, whatcha doin'? How come you're taking so long? Lunch is nearly over. Heeeey? What are you girls doing hiding behind those desks? What's going on?"

It was Chewy.

I **grabbed him** and shoved him back a few steps.

"SHHHHHHHHHHHH! I'm trying to get THAT," I said, pointing at the **killer grasshopper.**

"I need to get it off the lockers so that the girls can get to their stuff. I'm pretty sure I can make him jump out the window if I can just ..."

But Chewy had stopped listening. He seemed **hypnotised** by the grasshopper.

WANTED

6cm
5cm
4cm

6cm
5cm
4cm

ON TWO COUNTS OF FIRST-DEGREE PESTICIDE

YOU ARE FEELING VERY HYPNOTISED...

"Is it ... **p-p-p-poisonous?**"

"What? Poisonous? What are you talking about? Grasshoppers aren't poisonous!"

Chewy was looking at me now and nodding his head like **a maniac**.

"But they **can** be, Eric! I saw this nature show once and there was this grasshopper **plague** and they ate these crops but the crops had poisonous **nuclear waste gunk** on them and the grasshoppers became **mutants** and they started biting and eating people and the people that just got bitten turned into **zombies** with these big bug eyes and these big jaws that CHOMPED anything that got in their way

GRAINS...
GRAINS...

I HAVEN'T SEEN ANY MUTANT GRASSHOPPERS. HAVE YOU?

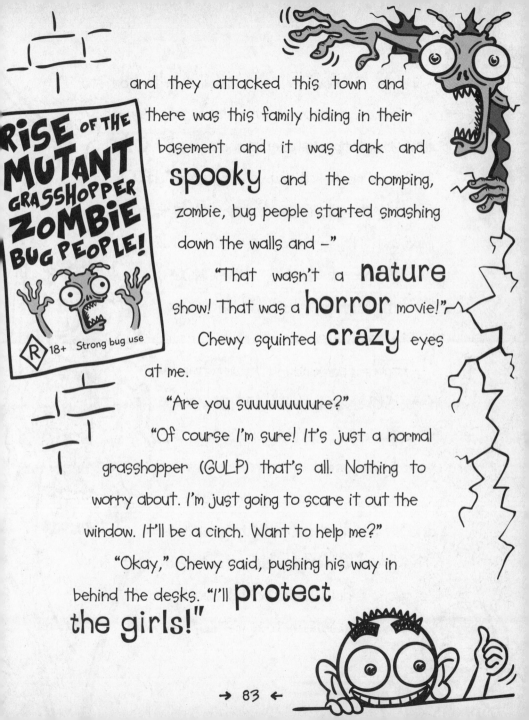

RISE OF THE MUTANT GRASSHOPPER ZOMBIE BUG PEOPLE!

R 18+ Strong bug use

and they attacked this town and there was this family hiding in their basement and it was dark and **spooky** and the chomping, zombie, bug people started smashing down the walls and –"

"That wasn't a **nature** show! That was a **horror** movie!"

Chewy squinted **crazy** eyes at me.

"Are you suuuuuuuuure?"

"Of course I'm sure! It's just a normal grasshopper (GULP) that's all. Nothing to worry about. I'm just going to scare it out the window. It'll be a cinch. Want to help me?"

"Okay," Chewy said, pushing his way in behind the desks. "I'll **protect the girls!**"

Of course I could have pointed out to Chewy that it might make more sense to protect the girls by standing in **front** of them rather than by hiding **behind** them, but I didn't have time. I had more important things to do.

I had a GIANT, POISONOUS, ZOMBIE-MAKING, KILLER GRASS-HOPPER to take care of!

I turned back round. It was still there. CURSES! I started creeping forward again. Closer. Closer. Clooooooooooser.

Now I was only an arm's length away. I reached out with the ruler. The grasshopper moved a foot and crouched down. He looked ready to spring. Someone behind me was whining.

I think it was Chewy. I pushed the tip of the ruler closer. My hand was **shaking.** The grasshopper's body dropped lower and its big, sharp, spiky back legs stretched out. I poked at it with the ruler a bit. "Shoo! Go on, shoo!"

YOU TALKIN' TO ME?

The grasshopper started to rock. Its goggle eyes looked **cold and angry.** Its jaws opened and shut. "Go on. Out you go, now. Shoo! I don't want to hurt you. The window's right there. Out you jump. Go on. You'll be free. Just a little jump now. Go on. Shoo!" I gently touched the tip of the ruler against one of the grasshopper's legs. It turned towards the window. And leapt.

STRAIGHT AT MY FACE!!!!!!!!!!

AAAAAAAAAAHHHHH!

My scream was drowned out by a bunch of other screams. Before I could stop them, my hands had turned into **helicopter blades** and were waving around my head on full throttle and my legs were doing a **warp speed** Riverdance!

Somehow after a few seconds I made myself stop.

Everything was **quiet.**

I checked the lockers. Nothing.

I checked the ceiling. Nothing.

I checked the floor. Nothing.

I looked all around the room. Nothing.

The grasshopper was gone! It was unbelievable. I'd done it! I'd chased the grasshopper out the window.

And the best part was that no one had seen my helicopter hands or **psycho Riverdance** because Chewy and the girls had ducked right down behind the desks. Not only that, they didn't hear my scream, because they were too busy screaming themselves.

What do you know? I couldn't believe it. For a moment there it looked like I was **a goner,** but then I ended up SAVING THE WORLD and being a BIG HERO!

"It's okay, everyone," I said. "You can all come out now. Problem solved. I've got **everything** under control."

Four heads poked up slowly from behind the desks. Four faces were **staring at me** like I was the Ninjarator and I'd just **saved** them all from Humungatroid. Sophie and Aasha and Li had their mouths open. They were obviously **so impressed** that they couldn't speak.

"Wow, Eric," Chewy said. "You really aren't afraid of grasshoppers at **all,** are you? I could **never** do that."

"It was nothing, really. You just need to know how to handle them. Nothing to be afraid of. Just had to get him to fly out the window, that's all."

Chewy **frowned.**

"He didn't fly out the window, Eric. He's on your collar."

"Yes, of course he is, but I ... HUH?"

I looked down at my collar. Two **angry zombie bug** eyes looked back at me.

AAAAAAEEEEE! EEEEEEEEEEEEEEK!

The grasshopper gets a **big fright.** It jumps. **At my face again!** I feel its wings and spiky legs beat and scratch against my nose and mouth. What if it bites me and I turn into a zombie!

I start doing a psycho Riverdance and helicopter hands encore, but this time it's a **high-octane** performance.

H.H.A.

HELICOPTER HANDS ARE NO LAUGHING MATTER, FOLKS.

→ 89 ←

One of my helicopter hands knocks the grasshopper away. **Yaaaaaaaaaaaaaaay!**

AND IT FALLS INSIDE MY COLLAR AND SLIDES DOWN! **Nooooooooooooooooo!**

Now it's bouncing and clicking around my chest and stomach like a spiky pinball! **Squueeeeeaaaal!**

I grab my shirt in both hands. **"Getitoff-getitoff-getitoff-getitoff-GET-IT-ORRRRRRFFFF!"**

I rip my shirt over my head and sling it across the room. It flies towards Chewy and the girls. They all scream. It hits Sophie Peters and wraps around her face.

Everybody screams again, only twice as loud. My eardrums feel like they are being cut with **a circular saw.** One of the screams is the highest note I think I've ever heard. It's coming from Chewy.

Sophie is wrestling with my shirt like it's a **feral cat** attacking her head. Finally she pulls it off and tries to fling it out the door. It doesn't quite make it.

Someone is standing in the doorway and the shirt lands at their feet.

The KILLER, MUTANT, ZOMBIE, PSYCHO, GRASSHOPPER **crawls** out!

The door-person bends down and picks it up in their hand. They bring it close to their face and smile.

"What are they **doing** to you, little guy? I bet what you'd like is a nice big tree."

The door-person is Meredith Murdoch. She turns and **gawks** at me.

And she's not alone. The lunch bell has gone and our whole class is lining up outside the room and gawking at me through the blinds. Sophie, Li and Aasha are gawking at me too. It's **definitely not** a "you're-our-**hero**-for-rescuing-us-from-the-killer-grasshopper-beast" sort of gawk. The one person not gawking at me is Chewy. But that's only because he's still got his eyes squeezed shut and is **hiding** behind the girls.

I'd been **beaten** by a grasshopper, **squealed** my lungs

out like a little kid, danced around like a **hyperactive clown,** **scared** a bunch of girls (and Chewy) half to death, and now I was standing shirtless in the middle of a classroom. I ask you, could it possibly get any **worse?**

"Hey, Vale!" It's Martin Fassbender with his face pushed between the blinds. "Love your Pony-Wony tattoo, man! Hahahahahahahahahahahaha!"

Yep. Apparently it could.

GOOD LUCK!

o•o•o•o•o•o•o•o•o•o•o•o•o•o•o

"Why couldn't the stupid thing just fly out the window? It was right **there!**"

Chewy and I were waiting at the bus stop after school.

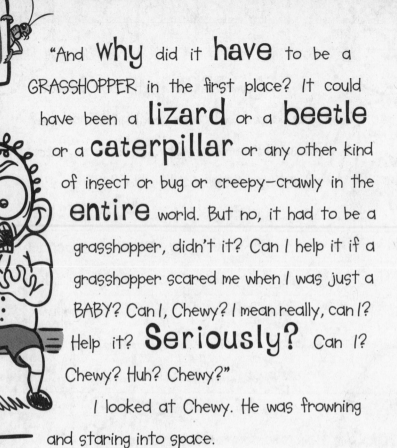

"And **why** did it **have** to be a GRASSHOPPER in the first place? It could have been a **lizard** or a **beetle** or a **caterpillar** or any other kind of insect or bug or creepy-crawly in the **entire** world. But no, it had to be a grasshopper, didn't it? Can I help it if a grasshopper scared me when I was just a BABY? Can I, Chewy? I mean really, can I? Help it? **Seriously?** Can I? Chewy? Huh? Chewy?"

I looked at Chewy. He was frowning and staring into space.

"Chewy, are you listening? Did you hear **anything** I just said?"

"What? Oh yeah, sure, Eric. Every word. But I'm just wondering what Wally Ramirez would've done in a situation like that."

BELIEVE!

WHAT!

"Wally Ramirez? Mr. Self-Belief? You wanna know what he would have done? He would've **magically** overcome his terror of grasshoppers by – wait for it! – **believing** in himself and then he would've given the grasshopper a great big cuddle and a kiss, and they would've become **best friends** forever, and then he would've taken it home and trained it to fetch his slippers!"

"Wow, you're great at making up Mr. Self-Belief stories, Eric!"

"Chewy, it's the **same** story EVERY time."

"No it's not."

"Yes it is and I'll **prove it** to you. When did your dad first start telling you these Mr. Self-Belief stories?"

YOU COMPLETE ME.

I'M IN A
TIGHT SPOT!

"Way back when I was just a little kid. Probably four or something."

I'M IN A
TIGHT SPOT!

"And how **often** did he tell them?"

"A couple of times a week. Maybe more."

"Okay. And when did he **stop** telling them?"

Chewy looked confused. "Stop?"

"Ooooooookaaaaaaaaaay. Good. Right. Well, that means your dad must have told you **hundreds** of Mr. Self-Belief stories."

"I guess so."

"Well, in how many of them did Wally Ramirez get into this **tight spot**

I BELIEVE!

where he had to do something really hard to get out of it, but he was **scared** and he thought he couldn't possibly do it?"

Chewy thought for **a second.** "All of them, I guess."

"Okay, good. Then tell me this. How many of those stories **didn't** end with Wally finally **believing** in himself, turning into Mr. Self-Belief, and actually doing the **exact** thing that he was scared of and thought he couldn't **possibly** do?"

Chewy frowned and bit his lip. He looked down at his hands and began counting on his fingers. Then he looked back up at me and nodded.

"None."

"Well, **there** you go. Do you see what I'm saying, then?"

I BELIEVE!

I BELIEVE!

"Yeah, I sure do, Eric – that Mr. Self-Belief is **totally awesome** and the **best superhero** ever!"

My head was starting to hurt.

BE AFRAID. BE *VERY* AFRAID.

"Hey, Eric, next time you see a grasshopper, you know what you should do? You should just tell yourself that you're not afraid and **you'll** be like Mr. Self-Belief and you'll just pick it right up!"

"Thanks heaps, Chewy. I'll be sure to remember that. But it's a bit late now, isn't it? I've already made a fool out of myself in front of everyone.

MAY THE HORSE BE WITH YOU. ALWAYS.

Oh, and let's not forget how I threw my shirt over Sophie Peters' head so I could show off my cool Precious Princess Pony-Wony Good Luck tatt."

IT ALL STARTED TO GO WRONG WHEN I GOT THAT FIRST TATTOO!

"You should be careful about getting any more tattoos, Eric. It might seem like a good idea **NOW,** but when you get older you mightn't think it's so cool, and then you're stuck with it. That's what my dad always says."

"What are you talking about? **It wasn't a real tattoo,** Chewy! And I didn't think it was cool! I just did it for Katie. It was supposed to wash off in water. But when I had my shower last night I forgot all about it. Probably needed soap and scrubbing as well.

POP

POP

→ 99 ←

I just **wish** I could explain all that to Sophie Peters."

"You really **like** her, huh, Eric?"

"Hey? What? Who? Sophie Peters? Me? Like? Are you kidding? What are you talking about? Me, like Sophie Peters? That's nuts! No way do I **like** Sophie Peters! I mean I don't **dis**like her or anything. There's nothing **wrong** with Sophie Peters. You know, as a **person.** But that's it. I don't **like** her and I don't **dis**like her. She's just Sophie Peters. And I'm just ... me. And that's all there is. Okay?"

"Sure, Eric. I get it. No problem."

Just then a **big shadow** fell over both of us. For a second I thought it was a **solar eclipse** but when I looked up it was just Robert "Big Bob" Falou.

"Hey," Big Bob said. "What's up, Eric? You don't look so happy."

Chewy shook his head.

EEEK! GRASSHOPPER BABY!

"He's not, Big Bob. You see, he's **crazy in love** with Sophie Peters, only she thinks he's a wimp on account of how he really likes all that Precious Pony-Wony stuff and also because of how he's **really scared** of grasshoppers and butterflies and all kinds of insects, bugs and creepy-crawlies – and even **babies.**"

MAMA.

"WHAT! That's not ... I didn't ... I'm not ..."

I ♥ SOPHIE PETERS

"Babies?" Big Bob said. "That's pretty weird."

Chewy looked at me and frowned.

"Yeah, Eric. Big Bob's right. That **is** pretty weird."

I shut my eyes and wondered how much **worse** it would get before it got **better.**

I wouldn't have to wait long to find out.

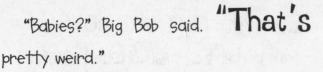

5. The League of Super Weirdos

The next day in class we started creating our very own superheroes. It was a lot of fun and it stopped me thinking about what happened yesterday. (Except when Martin Fassbender tried to **scare** me with this **stupid,** pretend, rubber grasshopper.) (Which only worked the first five or six times he did it.)

Anyway, by the end of the day we'd come up with a whole bunch of new superheroes to use in our superhero stories. Here's a sample:

(kidding)
turn over →

Inflato Man by Big Bob.

YOU'RE UNDER ARREST.

Description: Able to make himself any size he wants just by blowing into his special inflato/deflato-thumb. Can shrink to squeeze through small spaces or blow himself up into a giant blimp and escape danger just by floating away.

My Superhero Rating: More than hot air!

Sonic Maths Girl

by Li Wan and Sophie Peters.

Description: Secret identity – fashion model Tallulah Bling. She's quick and strong and can fly and zip around everywhere.

CRIME + PUNISHMENT = JUSTICE!

Plus she can do tricky maths calculations super fast in her head, which means she can work out things like exactly how long a speeding bullet will take to reach her. Has a special calculator that fires really long equations at the bad guys and gets them all confused. Wears a body suit covered in numbers and maths symbols.

$$(\sqrt{9} + (56 \div 8))^2 = \sqrt{81} + 91$$

I DON'T GET IT.

My Superhero Rating: Way too cool for school!

Captain Stench and The Ponginator by

Martin Fassbender and Tyrone Knowles. (Are you surprised?)

I STINK, THEREFORE I AM.

Description: Crime-fighting team that have a unique method of "exterminating" the bad guys. Mr. Winter calls it "inappropriate and unacceptable." Mr. Winter exterminates **them.**

My Superhero Rating: They stink!

Spewman and The Incredible Puke by

Martin and Tyrone. (Second effort.)

Description: Use your imagination.

My Superhero Rating: They're sick! (But not in a good way.)

The Amazing Mr. You-Can-Do-It by Chewy Rodriguez.

Description: A normal kid with the amazing name of Willy Robertson who

MY FRIENDS CALL ME CHUCK.

I AM ... AMAZING!

turns into an **amazing** superhero when **amazingly** he manages to convince himself that he can do **amazing** stuff. (I wonder where Chewy got **that amazing** idea from.)

My Superhero Rating: AMAZING!

MR. YCDI

Super Serenity Sister

by Saffron Blossom Jones.

Description: Triple **S** for short. Goes around spreading peace and love everywhere. Showers bad guys with her super incense and her super flower-power. This makes them all happy and friendly and they hug everyone and go home.

My Superhero Rating: PUH-LEEEEEEEEASE!

PEACE OUT!

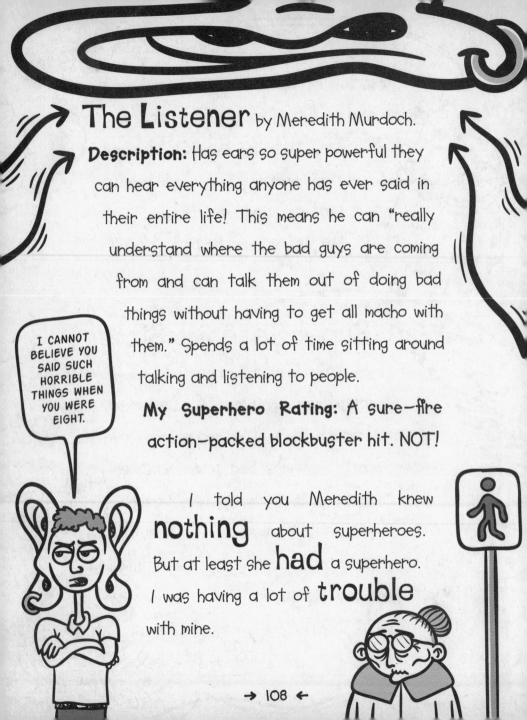

The **Listener** by Meredith Murdoch.

Description: Has ears so super powerful they can hear everything anyone has ever said in their entire life! This means he can "really understand where the bad guys are coming from and can talk them out of doing bad things without having to get all macho with them." Spends a lot of time sitting around talking and listening to people.

My Superhero Rating: A sure–fire action–packed blockbuster hit. NOT!

I told you Meredith knew **nothing** about superheroes. But at least she **had** a superhero. I was having a lot of **trouble** with mine.

I CANNOT BELIEVE YOU SAID SUCH HORRIBLE THINGS WHEN YOU WERE EIGHT.

Then I thought maybe I could use Secret Agent Derek "Danger" Dale because he already was a hero. **Cool!** I just needed to figure out a way to give him some sort of super power.

But what? And how?

I was still trying to work that out when Mr. Winter asked me to go to the copying room and get them to run off some more of our unit outlines. Apparently some **careless** people had lost theirs already. Me, for instance.

Anyway, while I was down there, staring at the **flashing light** of the photocopier and watching the sheets of paper spit out the end, I thought about Agent Dale inside that pyramid looking for Doctor MacEvilness.

YOO-HOO! DOC M?

Then I had an idea.

WHAT IF ...

Secret Agent Derek "Danger" Dale stepped over a not-so-mighty pile of dust that once was the Pharaoh Thikasabrikus and examined the rest of the chamber. There was some writing on the far wall. Luckily Agent Dale was an expert in ancient languages.

"Let's see. It says here ... *This is ... a SECRET door ... to a SECRET room ... but don't tell anyone ... because ... it's a ... SECRET!*"

Agent Dale pushed on the wall. A door swung open. It led into a SECRET room! Agent Dale had finally discovered the secret headquarters of the evil Doctor Evil MacEvilness!

"Seize him and take him to the Duplicatorium!" Agent Dale was grabbed by two armed guards. (That's because one-armed guards aren't so great at grabbing people.) They dragged Dale to the front of a strange machine.

"Welcome, Agent Dale. You're just in time to help me test out my most evil invention ever - the Duplicatorium! Not only can it copy *anything*, it can also re-size, repair and improve on the original. It's the ultimate photocopier! To demonstrate, I will make an evil copy of you who will then destroy the old you. Don't you just LOVE the Duplicatorium? Isn't it to DIE for? WHAHAHAHAHAHA!"

"You're mad, MacEvilness!"

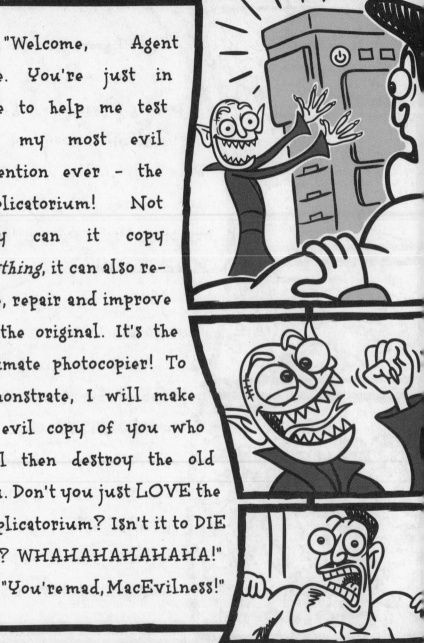

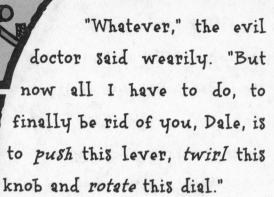

"Whatever," the evil doctor said wearily. "But now all I have to do, to finally be rid of you, Dale, is to *push* this lever, *twirl* this knob and *rotate* this dial."

A strange noise filled the room. Sparks shot from the Duplicatorium. It glowed red and shook.

"Wait a minute. Maybe that should have been *rotate* the lever, *push* the knob and *twirl* the dial. The energy flow is in chaos! The system is malfunctioning! It's going to explode! Ooops, my bad. Well, I really must fly ...

"Guards, carry me to the secret helipad!"

Agent Dale tried to stop them, but his body began to shake and tingle.

"What's happening to me? My body! It's changing! Is it possible ... that I ... am ... becoming ..."

ZZZZZZZZZZZZT!
WAAAAAAAAARP!
CLANK! POP!
BAAAAAVOOOOOOOM!

Biiiiiiiing!

"There you go, young man. Photocopying all done."

"What? Huh? Where?"

"Sorry to have to wake you up from your daydreaming, lovey, but Mr. Winter will be waiting for these."

I ran all the way back to the classroom, gave Mr. Winter the photocopying, raced to my desk and began writing.

By the time the bell went to go home, I'd found my superhero!

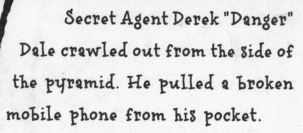

Secret Agent Derek "Danger" Dale crawled out from the side of the pyramid. He pulled a broken mobile phone from his pocket.

"Time for an upgrade," he said as he stretched out his arm and jabbed at the row of buttons on his wrist.

"Number of copies - One. Setting - Repair. Quality - Best."

He stared at the busted phone in his hand. A beam of light shone from his eyes and swept across it. Then he stared at his other hand and made a strange humming noise. A second, brighter light shone from his eyes and a brand new, top-of-the-range mobile appeared.

It rang.

"Agent Dale, is that you? Where have you been? We've been trying to contact you for hours."

"Sorry, Boss. Must have been out of range."

"Well, we've got a BIG problem. Evil Doctor Evil MacEvilness has been spotted heading to New York with an enormous roll of paper and a mountain of string. We think he might be planning to kidnap the Statue of Liberty! Your assignment, whether you choose to accept it or not, is to go to New York immediately, find out what he's up to and stop him. Do you copy?"

Agent Dale twirled the brand new phone in his hand and smiled to himself.

"Copy? I certainly do, Boss - like you wouldn't believe!"

And that was how Secret Agent Derek "Danger" Dale became ...

CAPTAIN COPIER!

Not bad, huh?

Wouldn't it be great to be able to copy anything and then change it and make it **better?** If I had that super power, you know what I'd do?

I'd make a copy of that day I tried to rescue Sophie Peters and the other girls and then I'd fix it up so that it worked out **exactly** how I wanted it to.

But I was just dreaming. I knew that I'd totally mucked up the one and only chance I'd ever get to be a hero.

Not true.

I was about to get **another chance** to totally muck things up all over again!

6. Eric Vale – Super Male to the Rescue! (Take Two)

The next day, when I was in the playground at lunchtime waiting for Chewy, I spotted Sophie Peters over by the old fig tree.

A boy was over there with her. It was Jarrod Dunn, the **biggest** kid in Year Seven. Quite a few people were standing around them. Sophie didn't look happy. She was a fair way off, but I could still hear her.

"It's not **funny.** Just give it back and **leave me alone!**"

Jarrod had Sophie's school hat and he was waving it about and holding it way up in the air. Every time Sophie tried to grab it back, he just pulled it away and **laughed** at her.

Sophie Peters was being picked on and **nobody** was doing anything about it!

Nobody except me, that is!

"Hey! Quit it! Leave her alone!"

Before I knew it, I was **charging** towards him.

ERIC VALE – SUPER MALE to the rescue – AGAIN!

Was I **mad?** He was much bigger than me! What was I going to do when I got there?

Wait. I know. I'll do the special Nuclear Ninjarator move! The one where he reaches out, grabs the bad guy by the arm, bends down, throws him over his shoulder and pins him on the ground with a foot to the chest. (Good thing for me I'd practised that **exact** move **heaps** of times on my pillow. At last all my hard work was going to pay off!)

I was almost there. It was **now or never.** I shouted out again. The crowd parted. Jarrod was right in front of me with a big **surprised look** on his face. Well, get ready, pal, because nobody picks on Sophie Peters while I'm around! Special Nuclear Ninjarator move coming up!

THIS PILLOW IS *DOWN!*

HA! FEATHERWEIGHT.

I shot out my hand – and someone **grabbed** it. HUH?

And **threw** me over their shoulder. WHA?

And **spun** me through the air. WHOOOOOA!

And **thumped** me on my back in the grass. OOOOOOOOMPH!

And **pinned me down** with a foot to the chest. ERRRRRRRRRGH!

Then everything stopped. Except my head, which kept right on spinning. I could hear laughing and clapping and **cheering.** I opened my eyes to get a look at the **giant thug** who'd thrown me around like a pillow and stomped their big hoof on my chest. And the giant thug I saw was ...

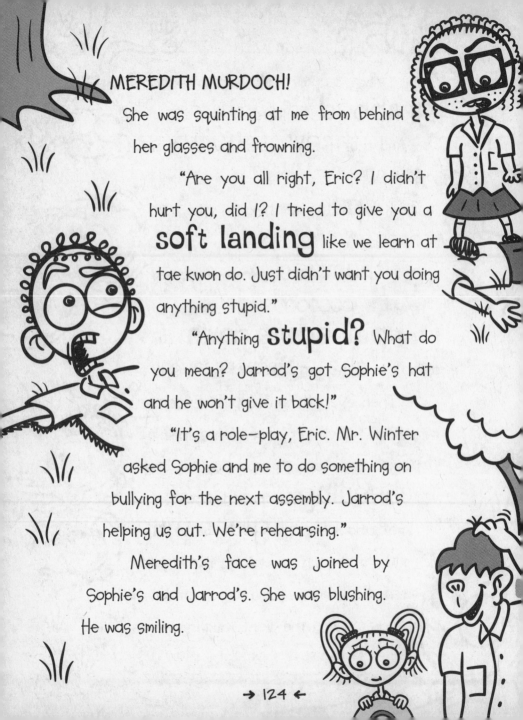

MEREDITH MURDOCH!

She was squinting at me from behind her glasses and frowning.

"Are you all right, Eric? I didn't hurt you, did I? I tried to give you a **soft landing** like we learn at tae kwon do. Just didn't want you doing anything stupid."

"Anything **stupid?** What do you mean? Jarrod's got Sophie's hat and he won't give it back!"

"It's a role-play, Eric. Mr. Winter asked Sophie and me to do something on bullying for the next assembly. Jarrod's helping us out. We're rehearsing."

Meredith's face was joined by Sophie's and Jarrod's. She was blushing. He was smiling.

"You okay, dude? Man, that was **SO** very cool. Like Meredith really owned you there. **Totally!**"

Fabulous. I groaned and tried to get up. I couldn't move!

"You want to take your foot off my chest now, Meredith?"

"**Oops.** Sorry. Forgot."

Everyone **cheered** and clapped and laughed some more when I stood up. Mainly laughed. Martin Fassbender was leading the way.

"Hey, Vale. I'm going to the tuckshop now. Want me to walk you across the playground? Wouldn't want you getting beaten up by any of the prep girls! Hahahahahahahahahaha!"

Just in case you missed it, that was another Fassbender **zinger**, folks!

I **stomped off** and found an empty bench waaaaaaaay on the other side of the playground and waited for Chewy.

That's **it!** From now on, I'm leaving all that hero stuff to guys like the Nuclear Ninjarator and Secret Agent Derek "Danger" Dale (aka Captain Copier). It's **no problem** for them. It's easy to be a hero when you're just a made-up character in a made-up story. It's a bit different if you have to live in the REAL WORLD like me. In the REAL WORLD, you can try your hardest to be a hero and just end up being a REAL-WORLD LOSER!

OH NO! I'VE BEEN MADE UP!

THERE, THERE.

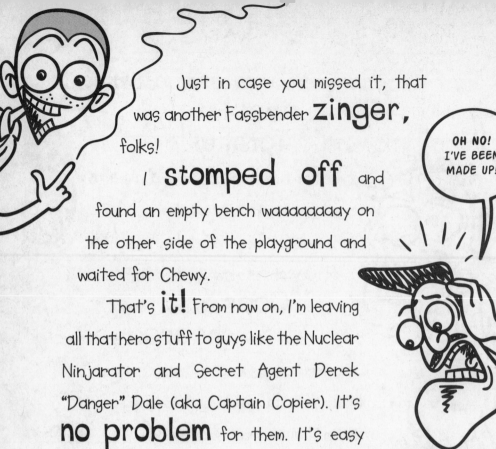

Yep, my mind was made up. Definitely, positively, **absolutely,** NO MORE HERO STUFF FOR ME!

"Hey, Eric! Guess what?"

OH NO! I'VE BEEN MADE UP!

It was Chewy. He was running across the playground and grinning like a **madman.** ⟶

"I just volunteered us to be the Trail Blazers for the HALL of HORRORS on Sunday! We're going to be HEROES!"

I could feel the blood draining from my face.

The Hall of Horrors was the **haunted house** that the Year Sevens ran every year at our big school fete and open day. No one below Year Five was allowed to go inside.

HEY! THIS TRAIL HAS A BLAZER ON IT!

That's why each year it was always a pretty **big deal** who would be **the first** of the new Year Fives to go through. The first two that did were called the Trail Blazers.

"You volunteered us to be Trail Blazers? What did you do that for?"

(Not that I was **scared** or anything. But when you've already come off **second-best** to a stuffed bear, a grasshopper and a **girl,** taking on something like the Hall of Horrors just seemed a little bit ... risky.)

"Well, I was in the tuckshop line and these Year Sevens were calling us Year Fives **chickens** because no one had their name down to be Trail Blazers.

CHICKENS, ARE WE? >BWARK!<

Anyway, Martin Fassbender comes along and he says, 'Well, I'm not afraid to do it, but I know someone who definitely **won't** do it – Eric Vale!' And then he just makes up some stupid story about you being so wimpy you get beaten up by girls. As if, huh, Eric! Anyway, so I said, 'You're **dead wrong,** Martin, 'cause Eric and me are volunteering to be the Trail Blazers!' And I got the Year Sevens to put both our names down, right there and then!"

I held my head in my hands.

"And the thing is, Eric, Jimmy Halabi told me there's nothing to worry about. He was a Trail Blazer last year and he said it's just a bit of the old assembly hall blacked out

AS IF BEING *DEAD* WASN'T ENOUGH. NOW I'M *INCORRECT!*

ERIC THE WIMP
BASED ON A TRUE STORY

R.I.P.
MARTIN FASSBENDER

and filled with curtains and screens to make a **sort of maze** plus some sound effects and masks and stuff. None of the Year Sevens is even allowed inside to scare you. Oh, and don't worry, Jimmy said there's definitely no grasshoppers or babies in there either. I asked him 'specially for you."

"I NEVER SAID I WAS AFRAID OF BABIES! What I **said** was, that when I was a baby I ... Okay, look, forget it. My name's down already, right, so it's done. I can't chicken out now, can I?"

"Awesome! And you know what they say, Eric. 'Go in Trail Blazers. Come out Legends!'"

Chewy was right. They did say that.
Hey, maybe this was my **big chance**
to wipe away my SUPER ZERO week.
All I had to do was **survive** the Hall
of Horrors.

Seriously, how hard could it be?

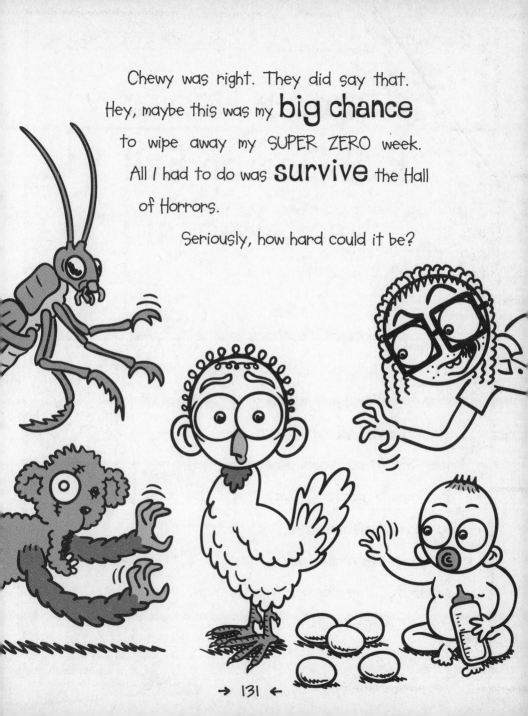

7. Captain Copier v Evil Doctor Evil MacEvilness!

We spent most of Thursday and Friday writing our superhero stories and using the library to do research for our real-life hero talks. We also made posters, cut-outs, mobiles and models of our made-up superheroes and decorated the classroom with them as part of 5W's open day display.

Of course Martin Fassbender couldn't wait to tell everyone about me getting **flattened** by Meredith (and he also managed to **scare** me three more times with that **stupid** rubber grasshopper **trick** of his) but the week still ended on a bit of a high.

What happened was, Mr. Winter said he really liked my Agent Dale/ Captain Copier character and GUESS WHAT? I got to spend most of Friday afternoon just working on the story!

When I'd left him, Agent Dale aka Captain Copier was headed to New York, **hot on the trail** of evil Doctor Evil MacEvilness ...

It was midnight when Secret Agent Derek "Danger" Dale landed his private state-of-the-art multi-million-dollar turbo-powered supersonic jet at the base of the Statue of Liberty.

"Hmmm," Agent Dale said to a security guard, "so *that's* the famous Statue of Liberty. Nowhere near as impressive as I thought it would be."

"That's because you're just looking at the base, sir. I'm afraid someone has stolen the *actual* statue itself. Just turned my back for six hours or so and

PFFT! It was gone!"

"CURSES! This looks like the evil doings of a certain evil Doctor Evil MacEvilness!"

"Well spotted!" the security guard said as he ripped off his disguise.

"Evil Doctor Evil MacEvilness!"

"In the FLESH, Agent Dale!"

"Yes, well, you really should have worn something under that disguise, then."

The evil doctor quickly grabbed an evil

cloak and wrapped it around his evil body.

"Igor, Boris, Rasputin, Dwayne! Seize him!"

Before he knew it, Derek "Danger" Dale was wrestled to the ground and tied in chains.

"I thought I'd seen the last of you, Agent Dale, but now that you are here, I suggest you listen closely. I have successfully kidnapped the Statue of Liberty, and my two most trusted and loyal servants are, at this very moment, guarding it in an abandoned warehouse. If I am not paid one billion dollars ransom IMMEDIATELY,

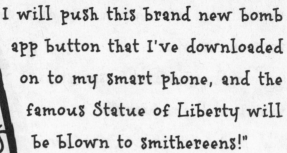

I will push this brand new bomb app button that I've downloaded on to my smart phone, and the famous Statue of Liberty will be blown to smithereens!"

"Along with your two most trusted and loyal servants?"

"Of course. And your point is?"

Agent Dale shook his head. "Some doctor you are. But how is any of that even *possible?* The Statue of Liberty is HUGE! How could you kidnap it without anyone noticing? How could you *move* it? And where would you find a warehouse big enough to store it in?"

"All excellent questions which, sadly, I just don't have the time to answer. Now, will you help me get my one-billion-dollar ransom or not?"

"Not on your life!"

"Have it your own way, Dale."

The evil doctor spoke into his smart phone.

"Hello? Most trusted and loyal servants? You might want to put your fingers in your ears. Ready? On the count of three, then. One. Two. THREE!"

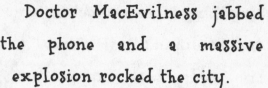

Doctor MacEvilness jabbed the phone and a massive explosion rocked the city.

"There. Perhaps next time when I kidnap the White House you'll pay up!"

"You'll never get away with this, MacEvilness!"

"Oh no? And how do you intend to stop me - from the bottom of the harbour?"

Agent Dale struggled to free himself.

"Don't knock yourself out, Dale. Those chains are unbreakable and that lock is unpickable. And *I*," the evil doctor said, pulling something from his pocket and holding it high above his head, "just happen to have the only key."

"*This* looks like a job for Captain Copier," Agent Dale mumbled to himself while his eyes secretly scanned the key. Then he stared down at his hands and hummed. A light flashed from his eyes. A second key appeared and he quickly closed his fingers around it.

"Gotcha!" Derek "Danger" Dale whispered.

"Are you prepared to meet your fate, Agent Dale?"

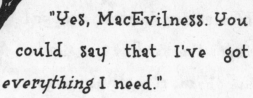

"Yes, MacEvilness. You could say that I've got *everything* I need."

"Igor, Boris, Rasputin, Dwayne! Throw him in the water!"

Secret Agent Derek "Danger" Dale's chained body splashed and sank into the cold water of the harbour.

Back on the surface Doctor MacEvilness and his evil sidekicks were about to board their evil airship when a masked figure with a body covered in strange plastic panels and arms filled with rows of flashing buttons stepped from the shadows.

"You're not going anywhere, MacEvilness."

"Who are *you*? Or should that be *what* are you? Are you going to a fancy dress party as a piece of office equipment? And how do you know my name?"

"I am Captain Copier - a very close friend of Secret Agent Derek 'Danger' Dale. He's told me all about you. Have you heard? Agent Dale almost had a nasty accident. Somehow he found

himself wrapped in chains at the bottom of this very harbour."

"How incredibly careless of him."

"Perhaps. But I'm sure you'll be pleased to hear that I have managed to rescue him and that he is now safe and sound."

Doctor MacEvilness let out a gasp.

"GASP! Well, that's a delightful story, crazy-office-equipment-man. But now, unfortunately, you die! Igor, Boris, Rasputin, Dwayne - open fire!"

A deadly hail of

bullets blasted their way towards Captain Copier. He poked at the buttons on his arm - and vanished!

"What? Where did he go?"

"Right over here, fellas."

Doctor MacEvilness and his four thugs spun round.

"You see, as well as the power to copy any object and repair, resize or improve it, I can also FAX myself to any location on earth AND as a special bonus, I can make some really lovely glossy prints. Pretty neat, huh?

I can also do THIS!"

Captain Copier hit the FULL FUNCTION EXTREME COPIER MODE button on his forehead. A big panel on his chest sprang open.

"Time for a Power Scan!"

A blinding bolt of light shot out. Doctor MacEvilness, Igor, Boris, Rasputin and Dwayne dropped their weapons and fell to their knees clutching their eyes.

"Don't worry, fellas, it's only temporary. In a few hours your sight will return to normal. Unfortunately though, all you'll be seeing is

the inside of a prison cell. My good friend the Police Chief and his boys will be here any second. I've already sent them an urgent fax, along with your group photo."

"You may think you've beaten me, Copier. But I've had the last laugh. The Statue of Liberty is no more!"

"That's where you're wrong, Doctor Mac E. You see, I took the precaution of purchasing this cheap, tacky, plastic souvenir of the Statue of Liberty from that cheap, tacky,

plastic gift shop over there."

Captain Copier ran his eyes over the souvenir and began pressing buttons.

"Let's see. Quantity - One. Quality - Best. Enlargement? I say 30,000 per cent should *just* about do it."

Captain Copier turned and stared at the centre of the empty base.

"Aaaaaaaaaaaand COPY!"

A full-sized Statue of Liberty rose into the night sky.

"Pity you and your boys can't see that, MacEvilness. It's truly spectacular, even if I do say so myself. Better than the original, in fact. Not only is the new Statue of Liberty rust-proof, but it also glows in the dark!"

- The End -

Be sure to stay tuned for more adventures of Secret Agent Derek "Danger" Dale
aka
CAPTAIN COPIER!
And remember, when Captain Copier's around, the action and excitement just MULTIPLY!

8. Mr. Self-Belief v The Oogily-Boogily Man!

By the time the weekend came around I was actually feeling pretty good about myself.

Mr. Winter had chosen my Captain Copier story as part of our main classroom display for the school fete and open day and everyone was talking about me and Chewy being the Year Five Trail Blazers. Lots of people wished us **good luck**. People like Sophie Peters!

Of course Martin reckoned we'd **chicken out,** and he kept making up these stupid stories to try to scare us. But it didn't work. I was feeling SUPER confident, and when I went over to Chewy's house on Saturday morning there was one thing I knew for sure – Mr. You-Can-Do-It himself would be POSITIVELY **bursting** with SELF-BELIEF too!

"We can't do it, Eric! The Hall of Horrors. No way. We just can't do it!"

Huh?

Chewy was sitting on his bed. **Shaking.**

"Chewy, what are you talking about, 'Can't do it'? You're the one who volunteered us to do it in the first place."

"But that was before."

BEFORE   AFTER

"Before what?"

"Before I knew about ... him."

"Him? Who him?"

"The Oogily-Boogily Man!"

"Hahahahahahahahahahahahaha! Yeah, good one, Chewy. You almost had me going there for a minute."

"No, Eric. I'm not joking. The Oogily–Boogily Man is REAL!"

"Riiiiiiiiiiiiiight. And by any chance is he related to the Spookily–Wookily Man or the Grumpily–Bumpily Man or the Ickily–Pickily Man?"

"Eric, I'm serious!"

He did look pretty serious. I pulled a chair out from Chewy's desk and sat down.

"Okay, then. So who is this Googily–Poogily Man, anyway?"

THERE'S A FOURTH BROTHER?

"Oogily-Boogily!"

"Yeah, right, fine ... him."

Chewy took a big breath. His eyes widened.

"He's this man, Eric, and he's got this big, ugly scar on his face and when he walks he sort of limps on one leg and draaaaaaaaaaaaaaaaaaaaaaaags the other one behind him."

"Sounds like a fun guy."

"No, Eric, he's not! What he does is, he goes around looking for fairs and stuff that have Haunted Houses in them, and then he breaks in when they're closed and he hides inside. And then ... he waits."

Chewy's eyes got a little bit bigger.

"He waits in his hiding place ... until the Haunted House opens. Then he creeeeeeeeeps out ...

and stands there **in the dark ...** waiting ...

and then the people start coming through ... and

he chooses one ... and he has this thing ..."

"He has a **thing?**"

"A **poem** thing that he says."

"Oh."

Chewy's eyes got even bigger and he made

his voice go **deep and creepy.**

> In the darkness, there I wait
>
> When you hear me, it's TOO LATE!

Chewy's eyes were looking like

spotlights now.

> Too late to SCREAM! Too late to RUN!
>
> Your Oogily–Boogily time HAS COME!

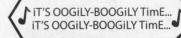

♪ iT'S OOGiLY-BOOGiLY TimE... ♪
iT'S OOGiLY-BOOGiLY TimE...

He stopped, **frozen** like a statue. I waited.

"AND THEN HE LEAPS RIGHT OUT AND GRABS YOU!"

Chewy's hands wrapped around my neck!

"AAAAAARRRRRGGGGGGH! Get off me, **you maniac!**"

"Sorry, Eric. I was just telling you about the Oogily-Boogily Man."

"Well, let me just tell you something, Chewy. That Oogily-Boogily thing is the **dumbest** thing I've ever heard. Okay? Not the **third**-dumbest or even the **second**-dumbest. The absolute, **gold-medal-winning,** first-place-getting-dumbest! Where did you get that crazy stuff from, anyway?"

RUBIN'S THE NAME
AND DUPIN'S THE GAME.

"My cousin Rubin told me all about it."

"Your cousin Rubin who's a couple of years older than us and used to go to our school? Your cousin Rubin who once told you that if you put two **big mirrors** on either side of your TV at just the right angle you could watch it in **3D?**"

"Yeah, and I still reckon we should try that, Eric. We just gotta find **one more** really big mir—"

"Chewy, he was pulling your leg then and he's doing it again now. There's no such person as the Oogily–Boogily Man. Rubin's just trying to **scare** you. And he's doing a **terrific** job!"

"But this time it's different, Eric. Rubin found out about the Oogily–Boogily Man from his dad. That's my uncle.

WOW! I'M ENTERING
THE THIRD DEMENTIA!

ACTUALLY, I'M A POLICE *CHEF.*

And he's **a policeman.** He's a Police Chief or something so he knows all about stuff like this."

"Look, Chewy. **If** – and I can't believe I'm about to actually say this – **if** there really was an Oogily-Boogily Man and **if** he really did **hide out** in Haunted Houses and grab people like you said, then don't you think it'd be all over the news?"

Uh-oh. Chewy was starting to do the **big eyes** again.

"That's what I thought too, Eric, but Rubin told me that the Oogily-Boogily Man first struck more than twenty years ago and back then it **was** all over the news. My uncle was one of the first policemen

THERE GO THOSE BIG EYES AGAIN.

I'M ON THE CASE.

on the case and he was there at the end too when the Oogily-Boogily Man was arrested and sent to **prison for life!**"

"Life in prison? Well, there you go. Problem solved!"

"No, Eric! There's more. Something happened."

"Wait, wait. Don't tell me. Let me guess. Just recently, the Oogily-Boogily Man happened to ... **escape!**"

"Hey, that's exactly right, Eric! But the police kept it **secret** because they didn't want to **panic** everyone. I was supposed to keep it secret too, but I had to tell you, Eric, didn't I? And you know what **else** Rubin said about the Oogily-Boogily Man?"

FINALLY! A MEANS OF ESCAPE.

THE LITTLE BOOK OF POLICE SECRETS

VOL XXIV

"Ummm, could it be that someone who looks **just** like him has been spotted in our local area recently?"

"Yes! A man with **a scar** on his face and a limp was spotted right near our school! And Eric, don't you see? All those little posters about the fete are up all over the place with 'Haunted House' on them in BIG LETTERS! The Oogily-Boogily Man MUST have seen them! That's why we can't be Trail Blazers tomorrow, Eric. And we have to **warn the others** as well!"

"Whoa! Back up! Okay, Chewy, listen to me now. This is **important.** We're NOT going to say ANYTHING to ANYONE about any stupid Oogily-Boogily Man. Okay?

KA-CHING.

HAUNTED HOUSE

Because I'm telling you, THERE IS NO SUCH PERSON!"

"But Rubin said ..."

"Look, who would you **believe** more? Rubin – who also told you that you wouldn't be allowed into Grade Five this year because you didn't make the minimum height requirement – or me, your **best friend** who has NEVER lied to you?"

YOU MUST BE AT LEAST THIS TALL TO ENTER GRADE FIVE

"You, Eric."

"Well then, here's the **truth.** The Oogily-Boogily Man is **not real.** Rubin just made it all up, okay? You can be a Trail Blazer tomorrow. You really can. You just have to **believe** it."

Chewy's head was bobbing slowly up and down but he still didn't look convinced.

Time to bring out the **big guns.**

"Don't you see, Chewy? It's like you're in your very own Wally Ramirez story! You're faced with something you think you can't do. But like Wally, if you start to really **believe** in yourself, you'll turn into Mr. Self-Belief and you'll just stroll right through that old Hall of Horrors as **easy as pie!**"

"Do you **really** think so, Eric?"

"I'm POSITIVE! 'Go in Trail Blazers. Come out Legends.' That'll be us! Are you with me, Chewy?"

Chewy sucked in a **big breath** and puffed it out again.

"I'm with you, Eric!"

Finally!

ZERO to HERO time coming up!

IT'S SO EASY BEING A PIE!

THREE THUMBS UP!

9. The Trail Blazers v The Hall of Horrors

The annual Moreton Hill Primary School Fete and Open Day **kicked off** at 11 am on Sunday morning. The Hall of Horrors opened its blacked-out doors at noon.

I was waiting at the entrance ten minutes early. Most of 5W and **plenty** of other kids were there too. Including Sophie Peters!

But not Chewy.

"Hey, Vale!"

Guess who.

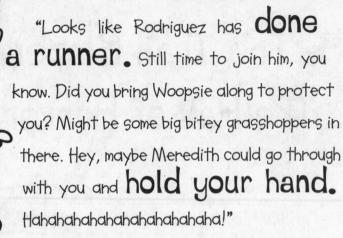

"Looks like Rodriguez has **done a runner.** Still time to join him, you know. Did you bring Woopsie along to protect you? Might be some big bitey grasshoppers in there. Hey, maybe Meredith could go through with you and **hold your hand.** Hahahahahahahahahahahaha!"

Martin Fassbender had **a million** of them. But it was like water off a superhero's back to me. I could do this.

Suddenly **a cheer** went up and a chant started.

"Woohoo! Choo-Choo! Woohoo! Choo-Choo!"

It was Chewy. He was bundled up in a puffy jacket with a scarf wrapped around his neck covering half his ears.

HEY! THAT'S DRY CLEAN ONLY!

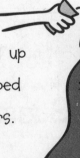

He looked a bit like **an emperor penguin.** More penguin than emperor.

"You cold or something?"

"Not really."

"Where've you been, anyway?"

"At the merry-go-round. Saw your mum and dad there so I took Katie for a ride on it. Man, that thing is scarier than it looks!"

Uh-oh. **Not a good sign.**

"Now, Chewy, remember what we talked about yesterday? How there's no such person as the Oogily-Boogily Man? I mean, think about it. If the police **really** believed that guy might be here at the fete, don't you think they'd have the place all **staked out?** Don't you think your uncle

MAKE IT STOP!!

WATCH ME DANCE, PA!

would be here **undercover** or something just in case?"

"My uncle **is** here."

"Yes, but it ... What?"

"My uncle is here, Eric. I just saw him at the Trash and Treasure stall talking with some other men."

Okay, that's not such a **big deal,** is it? I mean, Rubin does go to another school, but he used to go to Moreton Hill, and I know his family lives nearby. So why wouldn't his father be at our fete? All **perfectly** normal.

"Rubin's here too somewhere. I was talking to him. And, Eric, Rubin said that the Oogily-Boogily Man ..."

THIS IS OFFICER RODRIGUEZ. THE GOLDFISH IS IN THE AQUARIUM.

COPY THAT.

→ 164 ←

What was that thing my mum was always saying? That's right. I remember. "GIVE ME STRENGTH!"

SIDE SPLITTING. NOT AS FUNNY AS I'D ANTICIPATED.

"High Noon, everyone! Where are our two Year Five **victims** ... Er, I mean **guinea pigs** ... Er, I mean Trail Blazers?"

DID SOMEONE SAY 'HIGH NOON'?

It was one of the Year Seven boys being **side-splittingly humorous.**

Chewy and I moved to the front of the queue. A pretty big crowd had gathered.

"First of all, according to workplace health and safety regulations," the Year Seven boy said, "you both must sign this **complicated** legal document so we don't get sued if something **horrible** and **nasty** happens to you in there."

TAKE THAT!

I rolled my eyes at him. Chewy and I signed the "complicated legal document." It was just a **blank** piece of paper with "IT'S NOT OUR FAULT!" scribbled on it.

"Okay. You ready to **rumble?**"

Chewy and I nodded. We walked over to the entrance. Two Year Seven girls were waiting there. As we got closer one said, "Hey, Rach, guess what? Someone broke into the school last night, but they didn't find anything missing or damaged. **Weird, huh?**"

IN CASE OF TRESPASSING BREAK WINDOW

What? I looked at Chewy. He was waving at the crowd. I don't think he heard. Just as well. I mean, it would be just like him to hear something like that and start thinking that maybe it was ... that **certain** made-up

imaginary person that we're not going to
mention ever again ... who broke in to the
school and that the reason nothing was
taken or damaged was because ... that
certain made—up imaginary person
didn't actually come to steal or wreck
anything, but only broke in to **hide**
out in the Hall of Horrors overnight
and wait there in the dark for their
first victims to come through,
which ... in this case ... would be ... the
Trail Blazers ... aka ... US. Yeah. That
would be **just** the sort of **crazy**
thing Chewy would think.

One of the Year Seven girls pulled
back the curtain to the entrance.
"Good luck," she said
with a big smile. "Rather you than me!"

Chewy and I stepped inside. The curtain closed behind us. It was just us and the Hall of Horrors.

At least, that's what I was hoping.

At first I couldn't see anything at all.

"Let's just stay here for a bit, Chewy, until our eyes get used to the dark, okay?"

"Okay, Eric."

I waited.

I began to see some shapes. I could make out Chewy fiddling with his scarf beside me. Further down the passageway there were curtains on both sides with some not-so-spooky-looking masks pinned to them.

Actually, to tell you the truth, it was a bit of a let-down. I really thought the Year Sevens could've done a lot better job of blacking out the hall to stop the light ...

BAAAAAAAAANG!

A door SLAMMED shut behind us.

Okay. I admit it. My heart had just tried to jump out of my mouth. It would have made it, too, if my teeth hadn't got in the way!

Now it was **pitch black**.

I stood still to let my eyes adjust again.

They didn't.

I held my hand up in front of my face to check that I could see it.

I couldn't.

DILATED PUPILS

I shut my eyes to see if it made any difference.

It didn't.

All riiiiiiighty, then.

"Whoa. Pretty dark, huh, Chewy? But don't worry, just follow me. I got a good look before that door shut, and it just goes straight ahead for a bit and then turns around to the right. Okay, let's go."

DON'T LOOK AT ME. I CAN'T SEE SQUAT.

I stuck one hand out in front of me and trailed the other hand along the curtain beside me. I was taking little, slow steps. When I reached the end of the first passageway I turned right ...

HEY! I'M ROTTIN' HERE! I'M ROTTIN' HERE!

STRAIGHT INTO A ROTTING CORPSE!

—EEP!

I jumped back and made a squeaking noise in my throat like a strangled hiccup.

"It's okay, Chewy. It's nothing. Just some glow-in-the-dark dead body thingy. I'll turn it around so you don't even have to see it. There. Okay, watch out. We've got quite a few skeletons coming up."

I made my way past a jumble of cardboard and styrofoam skulls and bones until the passageway swung around to the left.

I was just starting to move a little bit faster when ...

SOMETHING ATTACKED MY FACE!

Eeeeeek! It was another GIANT grasshopper! No, it was a SWARM of

AHEAD

YOU WERE WARNED.

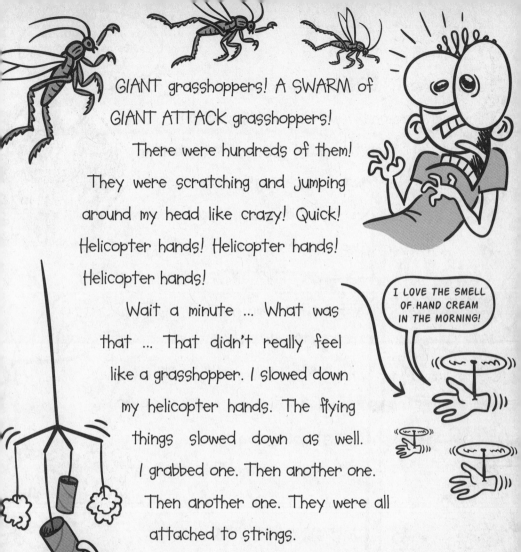

GIANT grasshoppers! A SWARM of GIANT ATTACK grasshoppers!

There were hundreds of them! They were scratching and jumping around my head like crazy! Quick! Helicopter hands! Helicopter hands! Helicopter hands!

Wait a minute ... What was that ... That didn't really feel like a grasshopper. I slowed down my helicopter hands. The flying things slowed down as well. I grabbed one. Then another one. Then another one. They were all attached to strings.

Ha! It was just a stupid mobile made of scrunched-up paper and old toilet rolls! How pathetic!

I LOVE THE SMELL OF HAND CREAM IN THE MORNING!

I CAN'T CHANGE WHAT I AM.

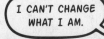

As if **that** was going to fool anyone! I warned Chewy about it, even though he was probably short enough to walk right under it.

I kept on going. Up ahead were two doors outlined in glow paint. One had "THIS WAY" written on it. The other one had "DANGER! DO NOT OPEN! BEWARE THE BEAST!"

"Beast?" I said over my shoulder to Chewy with a bit of a laugh. "Sure. I just gotta see this."

I opened the "Beast" door.

ROOOOOOAAAAAARRRRRR!

I slammed the door shut.

Okay, that was just a sound effect. A really LOUD and UNEXPECTED and really REAL-SOUNDING sound effect!

"Aaaah, okay, Chewy, let's just take **this** one then," I said.

On the other side of the door, the passageway seemed to widen out. It was like we were in a big black hole surrounded by curtains. I couldn't figure out which way we were supposed to go.

"This is a bit weird, Chewy. Is there another door or a gap in the curtains near you? Chewy? Did you hear me? Chewy?"

Suddenly I realised. Chewy hadn't said a word for ages.

"Chewy, are you there?"
I tried it a bit **louder.**

"Chewy? If you can hear me, say something."

Nothing. Just stillness and blackness.
"Say **anything.**"

IT'S A CELESTIAL RARITY, FOR SURE. A BIG BLACK HOLE SURROUNDED BY CURTAINS.

Where was he?

Why didn't he answer?"

"CHEWY! IT'S ERIC! IF YOU CAN HEAR ME, SAY SOMETHING!"

Okay, he **must** have heard that.

Nothing. Not a sound. Except ...

Did I just hear some floorboards creaking? Probably just another stupid sound effect. It can't be another person, because no one else is allowed in until the Trail Blazers are finished. Maybe it was Chewy.

"Chewy! That you?"

Nothing.

Wait a minute. What was that? That noise. Something bumping.

CHEWY, WHERE ARE YOU...

GIVE IT UP, KID. I STARTED CREAKING FOR ATTENTION 27 YEARS AGO. NOBODY LISTENS.

CREAK!

BUMP!

And that one? A scraping sound. It was like a CLUMP followed by a SCRAAAAAAPE. There it goes again! CLUMP and SCRAAAAAAPE. CLUMP and SCRAAAAAAPE. CLUMP and SCRAAAAAAPE. What **is** that? Oh, I know! It sounds **just** like someone limping and then dragging their ... other leg ... behind them ...

I spun round. It stopped.

No. No, it couldn't be. Don't be stupid. You're not a baby. You don't believe in the Tooth Fairy, do you? Still ... it's a bit weird how Rubin's father was hanging around and he's a policeman and everything ... and how someone broke in to the school last night but didn't take anything. Probably just coincidences. Yeah, that's all they are, just coin–

THE ADVENTURES OF **CLUMP** AND **SCRAPE**

Wednesday nights at 8

I'VE *SOILED* MYSELF!

Someone was breathing in the darkness! It was like Darth Vader with a really bad chest infection!

Then a voice growled from the shadows.

IN THE DARKNESS, THERE I WAIT!

Huh? What?

WHEN YOU HEAR ME, IT'S TOO LATE!

No. That's not right. It can't be.

TOO LATE TO SCREAM! TOO LATE TO RUN!

It's not real. It's just a recording.

YOUR OOGILY-BOOGILY TIME ... HAS COME!

I stepped backwards. I bumped into something. A hand flopped on to my shoulder! Fingers curled around my neck.

I was being oogily-boogled!

AAAAAARGGGH!

I charged straight ahead at full speed. I tore through curtains, smashed past skeletons, crashed over partitions and burst out the exit into the blinding sunlight.

GAAAAAAH!

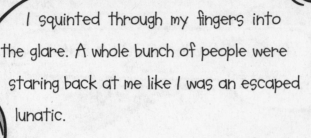

I squinted through my fingers into the glare. A whole bunch of people were staring back at me like I was an escaped lunatic.

"Oogily-Boogily!   Oogily-Boogily!" I shouted, pointing into the Hall of Horrors. "Oogily-Boogily! Oogily-Boogily!"

A whole bunch of people stared back at me like I was an **armed** and **dangerous** escaped lunatic.

"The Oogily-Boogily Man – he's in there! I heard him. He said his thing! He tried to get me! He grabbed my neck! I only just ..."

I looked around the crowd.

"Wait. Where's Chewy?"

Meredith Murdoch answered. "He hasn't come out yet. You were first."

"What? You mean Chewy's still somewhere inside ... with the Oog—"

I untangled a strip of black curtain from around my shoulders, kicked a busted cardboard skeleton off my foot and charged back towards the exit.

Just as Chewy wandered out blinking. And smiling.

I grabbed him by the shoulders.

"Chewy! Where did you go? **What happened?** Why didn't you answer me in there? Did you see him? Did you see the Oogily-Boogily Man? Are you okay?"

Chewy looked at me blankly. Then he reached up and pulled two buds from his ears.

POP!

"Sorry, Eric. What was that? Didn't hear a word you just said. I've been listening to one of Mum and Dad's audiobooks. **Make Your Fears Your Friends - Turning Negative Thoughts into Positive Actions!** It's really excellent!"

What? Nothing was making any sense. Was I just dreaming this? I turned round. The crowd seemed real enough. Some were laughing their heads off. Some looked confused. Others (mainly Year Sevens) looked kind of angry. One of the crowd was pointing at me and grinning like a maniac. It was Martin Fassbender.

"Hey, Vale! **Love** the necklace!"

What was **that** all about? Had Martin finally gone completely loopy?

ZING

→ 182 ←

I looked down at my chest.

WHAAAAAAAAAAT?

WOOPSIE BEAR was dangling from my neck by his long orange orangutan arms!

Of course, I knew then that none of it was real. It was all JUST SOME CRAZY DREAM!

○●○●○●○●○●○●○●○●○●

Okay, it wasn't all just some crazy dream. More like a **nightmare.** Except I wasn't asleep.

"What happened in there? Where did you go?"

I'd dragged Chewy away from all the laughing and pointing and staring, to try and get some answers.

WE WANT ANSWERS, CHEWY.

"Nowhere. When we got inside, you said to wait until we could see better. While I was waiting I put in my earphones and started listening to **Make Your Fears Your Friends - Turning Negative Thoughts into Positive Actions!** Then it went **really** dark and I waited for you to give the signal to start. I waited for ages. How come you didn't say anything, Eric?"

"I **did** say something! I said **heaps** of things! But you didn't hear **any** of them, because you were too busy listening to **Making Your Friends Afraid** or whatever it is!

I BELIEVE!

Weren't you **frightened** at all?"

"Not really. I just concentrated on turning my 'negative thoughts into positive actions' and I walked right through. Just like Mr. Self-Belief!"

"The Beast didn't scare you?"

NAH, I CAN HOLD IT.

"Oh, I didn't open **that** door, Eric. It said there was a Beast behind it."

"Well, what about the stupid paper and toilet roll thing hanging from the ceiling?"

"Huh? The what?"

"Oh, right ... then what about all the creaking and thumping and scary breathing noises? And what about the poem? What about the creepy voice saying the Oogily-Boogily Man poem?"

APPROXIMATE DISTANCE BETWEEN CHEWY AND MOBILE: 3 METRES.

COME ON! I'M SITTING ON A GOLD MINE HERE!

"Didn't hear any of that, Eric. But it must have been a recording, because the Oogily-Boogily Man isn't real. He's made up. Just like the Tooth Fairy. Except he doesn't leave money when your teeth fall out."

"Well, I know that! That's what I told **you!** But I didn't think you believed me!"

"Well, I kind of didn't, not until Rubin said the same thing."

"Rubin?"

YOU CAN EASILY HANDLE THE TRUTH!

"Yeah, after you left on Saturday I told my dad what Rubin said about the Oogily-Boogily Man and he rang my uncle, and my uncle made Rubin tell me the truth. Guess what. Rubin is still friends with some of our Year Seven boys and they just made up that Oogily-Boogily

story together to try to scare us so
we wouldn't make it through the Hall
of Horrors."

"What! If you **knew** all that
when you got here, why didn't you
tell **me?**"

"I tried, Eric, but you said you
didn't care what Rubin said and then
you told me not to mention a ... certain
made-up imaginary person ... or talk
about that ... **certain** made-up
imaginary person ... ever again. So I didn't."

I groaned and held my head to stop it
from exploding.

"Okay, okay, I get **all** that. But who
grabbed my shoulder and tried to strangle me
in there? And how did I end up with Woopsie
Bear around my neck?"

OH NO!
I'VE BEEN
MADE UP!

"Oh, that's easy. I put him there."

"WHAT? YOU? HOW? WHY!"

"Katie gave him to me at the merry-go-round. She said he would protect me from all the spooky-spooks in the Hall of Horrors. Isn't that cute? He was tucked under my jacket when I went inside. Anyway, I was doing great 'turning negative thoughts into positive actions' so when I bumped into you in the dark, I thought maybe you could use Woopsie more than me. That's when I patted you on the shoulder – just to let you know it was me – and velcroed Woopsie's arms around your neck. Did he help at all?"

YOUR WOOPSILY-BOOPSILY TIME ... HAS COME!

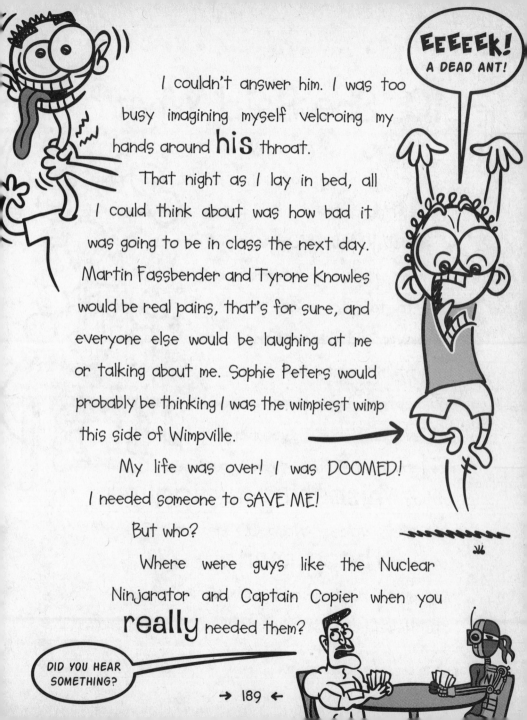

I couldn't answer him. I was too busy imagining myself velcroing my hands around **his** throat.

That night as I lay in bed, all I could think about was how bad it was going to be in class the next day. Martin Fassbender and Tyrone Knowles would be real pains, that's for sure, and everyone else would be laughing at me or talking about me. Sophie Peters would probably be thinking I was the wimpiest wimp this side of Wimpville.

My life was over! I was DOOMED! I needed someone to SAVE ME!

But who?

Where were guys like the Nuclear Ninjarator and Captain Copier when you **really** needed them?

EEEEEK! A DEAD ANT!

DID YOU HEAR SOMETHING?

10. She Said What?

The next day I timed it so I got to school **just** before the bell rang. That way I didn't have to talk to anyone in the playground. Then I went straight into class, sat down and kept my eyes on my desk. But everyone else's eyes were on me. I could feel them. And I could hear lots of **whispering** and **giggling.**

"Hey, Vale ... WooooOOOoooooOOOooooooo ... I think the **boogyman** might be coming to get you! Quick, run home and get Woopsie before it's too late! Hey, I hear they made Rodriguez a Trail Blazer.

So what did they make you? A **FAIL** Blazer or a Trail **FIZZER**? Hahahahahahahaha!"

Martin and Tyrone were having a snort-a-thon behind me. I suppose I was just going to have to get used to it.

Then Mr. Winter told everyone to be quiet and settle down and I took a chance and looked up. Meredith Murdoch was twisted round and **gawking at me** from her seat up the front. What was her problem?

"Rightio, everyone," Mr. Winter said. "Time to commence our hero talks."

Brilliant! Just what I **didn't** need. To hear all about people who were THE TOTAL OPPOSITE OF ME! →

"Who'd like to volunteer to go first?"

BIZARRO ERIC

Meredith Murdoch stuck up her hand. (Who else?)

Mr. Winter took a seat down the back of the room near Martin and Tyrone. Meredith was out the front of the class holding a bunch of cue cards. She pulled an elastic band off them. Then she stood there for **ages** without saying anything. Meredith Murdoch was being **even weirder** than usual!

"Whenever you're ready, Meredith," Mr. Winter said.

Yes, Meredith — you want to move it along a bit? We'll all be in Year Six soon!

At last she looked up and bit her lip. Then **guess what.** She wrapped the elastic band back around her cue cards and put them on the desk in front of her.

Huh?

THIS BRAIN IS A BIT TOO TIGHT.

"We're supposed to talk about real people who are **brave.** Real-life heroes. Well, I **was** going to talk about my great-great-grandfather Arthur Murdoch, who was very brave and fought in a war and won some medals, but I changed my mind."

What? Changed your mind? Just now? How dumb is that?

"Heroes are people who do brave things to help someone else, but that doesn't mean they don't get **scared** too. How can you do something brave unless you're afraid of doing it in the first place? That's what being brave means, doesn't it? Doing something even if it frightens you? That's why I think a lot of superheroes aren't really **brave** at all.

DOES THIS MEAN I HAVE TO CHANGE MY NAME?

CAPTAIN BRAVE

STEEL? HA! TRY BEING MADE OF PAPER.

I mean, is it really that brave to stand in front of a bullet if you're made of **steel?** I don't think so."

HELLO, I'M MEREDITH MURDOCH AND YOU'RE WATCHING "CRAZY TALK."

What was Meredith going on about? This was **crazy** talk!

"So that's why, for my presentation today, I've decided to talk about someone who maybe most of you wouldn't think is brave or a hero at all. But I think you'd be wrong."

THANKS, BUBBLES. THAT WAS A HARD DAY'S SWIM.

All right. Heeeeeeeeeeere we go. I bet she's going to talk about her **pet goldfish,** Bubble Cheeks, bravely rescuing a beetle that fell into its goldfish bowl or something.

"The subject of my hero talk is ... Eric Vale."

Him! What did he ever ... Wait, did she just say **Eric Vale?** But that's **my** name.

Suddenly everyone was talking and turning round and **staring** at me, then back at Meredith, then me, then Meredith, then me. What was going on? Was this some kind of sick **joke** or something?

"Settle down, please, everyone," Mr. Winter said. "Thank you. Right, keep going, Meredith. You've certainly got our attention and you're doing just fine."

"Okay, here's why I chose Eric." Meredith took a deep breath.

I took an even deeper one.

"First of all, last Tuesday, Li and Sophie and Aasha couldn't get to their lockers because there was a grasshopper there and they were frightened of it, so they asked Eric to help them."

What was she bringing **that** up for? I wanted everyone to forget that day!

"Even though Eric is really scared of grasshoppers (which is **pretty dumb,** because they're harmless and cute), he still tried to help out. I think he was brave to do that."

HUH? CUTE? *ME?*

Huh? Brave? **Me?**

"Then, on the very next day, Eric thought Sophie was being bullied by Jarrod Porter from Year Seven.

Of course it wasn't true, because they were just doing a bullying role-play, but Eric thought it was real and he came running in to try to help Sophie."

I looked over at Sophie Peters. She'd gone about the same colour as Mr. Winter's hair.

"It was pretty funny for Eric to run in like that, but it was **brave** too, because we all know that if Jarrod really was a bully he would have **squished** Eric like a grape."

Grape! That's a bit much! Plum, maybe.

I BEWIEVE.

IS IT A CRIME TO **BOOGIE, MAN?**

"And then, just yesterday at the school fete and open day ..."

Oh no! Not that! Please, don't mention that! Give me a break!

"Eric thought there was some sort of **boogyman** in the Hall of Horrors, which is something you'd think only a little kindergarten kid would ever believe."

Gee, thanks, Meredith! Don't build me up too much, will you?

"But that doesn't matter. What matters is that Eric really believed it and then when he thought that Chewy was still inside and might be in trouble, he didn't worry about any boogyman being there, he just started to run back in to save him. I thought that was a really **brave** thing to do too."

HOLD ON, CHEWY!

Chewy turned round in his seat and gave me two **thumbs up** and a giant grin.

"My point is," Meredith said, "that even though you could say that everything Eric was afraid of was either pretty dumb or not real, the 'being afraid' part was real for Eric. But he still tried to help. Three times in one week. Isn't that the sort of thing heroes do? And Eric didn't even have an iron **robot suit** or super powers or a **magic wand** or anything like that to help him. So that's how come I chose him for my hero talk today. That's all. Thank you."

Meredith sat down quickly and stared at her desk. Everything went quiet for a second. Then Big Bob let out a WHOOP!

SHAZAM!

and started **clapping** like crazy. Then Chewy joined in, and so did Li and Aasha and Sophie and soon everyone was clapping and **cheering** and looking round at me. A few people patted me on the back. Even Martin Fassbender was slapping his hands together slowly and sort of smiling a bit when he said, "Not bad, Vale, but I bet you couldn't have done it without Woopsie!"

In the end there was so much noise I thought we would get in trouble. But Mr. Winter just leaned back on his chair and smiled. And then he joined in! And then it got **even better.**

At morning tea, Li Wan, Aasha Alsufi and Sophie Peters(!) each gave me a big hug

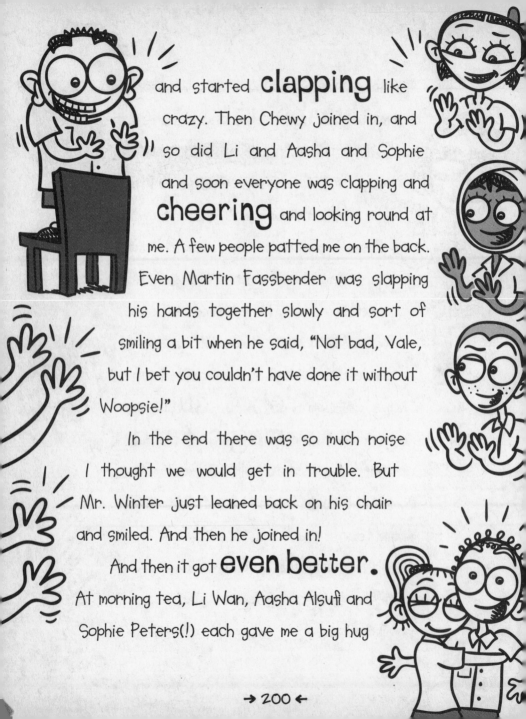

for trying to help them out with the grasshopper and they called me a real SUPERHERO!

BEST. DAY. EVER!

But don't worry. I wasn't kidding myself or getting too carried away. It was great what Sophie and Li and Aasha said, but I knew that they were just being nice — like always.

I'm nothing like a superhero. Not really. Real superheroes do stuff that I could never do in a trillion years.

Like **real** superheroes take on scary beasts and **monsters.**

And **real** superheroes protect innocent people from danger.

And best of all, when you're facing **doom** and **disaster,** and when you desperately need them, real superheroes somehow turn up out of nowhere, to save you.

Yep. No doubt about it, **real** superheroes **totally rock!**

And the very first chance I got, that's **exactly** what I told Meredith Murdoch.

(Who else?)

ERIC VAL

~~LOSER~~
~~WIMP~~
HERO ✓✓